THE CASE
OF THE
GYPSY GOOD-BYE

THE CASE
OF THE
GYPSY GOOD-BYE

AN ENOLA HOLMES MYSTERY

NANCY SPRINGER

PHILOMEL BOOKS

AN IMPRINT OF PENGUIN GROUP (USA) INC.

PHILOMEL BOOKS
A division of Penguin Young Readers Group.
Published by The Penguin Group.
Penguin Group (USA) Inc., 375 Hudson Street, New York, NY 10014, U.S.A.
Penguin Group (Canada), 90 Eglinton Avenue East, Suite 700, Toronto, Ontario M4P 2Y3,
Canada (a division of Pearson Penguin Canada Inc.).
Penguin Books Ltd, 80 Strand, London WC2R 0RL, England.
Penguin Ireland, 25 St. Stephen's Green, Dublin 2, Ireland (a division of Penguin Books Ltd).
Penguin Group (Australia), 250 Camberwell Road, Camberwell, Victoria 3124, Australia
(a division of Pearson Australia Group Pty Ltd).
Penguin Books India Pvt Ltd, 11 Community Centre, Panchsheel Park,
New Delhi - 110 017, India.
Penguin Group (NZ), 67 Apollo Drive, Rosedale, North Shore 0632, New Zealand
(a division of Pearson New Zealand Ltd).
Penguin Books (South Africa) (Pty) Ltd, 24 Sturdee Avenue, Rosebank,
Johannesburg 2196, South Africa.
Penguin Books Ltd, Registered Offices: 80 Strand, London WC2R 0RL, England.

Library of Congress Cataloging-in-Publication Data
Springer, Nancy.
The case of the Gypsy good-bye / Nancy Springer.
p.   cm. — (An Enola Holmes mystery)
Summary: After fourteen-year-old Enola Holmes seeks the missing Duquessa del
Campo in the seedy underbelly of nineteenth-century London, she finally
reaches an understanding with her brothers, Sherlock and Mycroft.
[1. Kidnapping—Fiction.   2. Brothers and sisters—Fiction.   3. Self-realization—Fiction.
4. Characters in literature—Fiction.   5. London (England)—History—19th century—Fiction.
6. Great Britain—History—19th century—Fiction.   7. Mystery and detective stories.]   I. Title.
PZ7.S76846Cari   2010
[Fic]—dc22   2009027141

ISBN 978-0-399-25236-5
1   3   5   7   9   10   8   6   4   2

To my mother

ALSO BY NANCY SPRINGER

THE ENOLA HOLMES MYSTERIES

The Case of the Missing Marquess
The Case of the Left-Handed Lady
The Case of the Bizarre Bouquets
The Case of the Peculiar Pink Fan
The Case of the Cryptic Crinoline

THE TALES OF ROWAN HOOD

Rowan Hood, Outlaw Girl of Sherwood Forest
Lionclaw
Outlaw Princess of Sherwood
Wild Boy
Rowan Hood Returns, the Final Chapter

THE TALES FROM CAMELOT

I am Mordred
I am Morgan le Fay

Ribbiting Tales

JULY, 1889

"MISTER SHERLOCK, I'M THAT GLAD TO SEE YOU, I am, and that obliged . . ." Mrs. Lane, faithful Holmes family servant, who has known the great detective since he was a boy in short pants, cannot keep the quaver out of her voice or the tears out of her dim old eyes. ". . . that obliged to you for coming . . ."

"Nonsense." Shrinking, as usual, from any display of emotion, Sherlock Holmes studies the dark woodwork of Ferndell Hall. "I welcome the opportunity to visit my ancestral home." Dressed in summertime country attire—beige linen suit, lightweight tan kidskin boots and gloves, deer-stalker cap—he lays the gloves and hat on the parlour table, as well as his stick, and proceeds at once to business. "Mr. Lane's telegram was rather enigmatic. Pray, what is so odd about this package you hesitate to open?"

Before she can answer, into the parlour hurries her husband, the white-haired butler, with considerably less than his usual dignity. "Mister Sherlock! How good of you!" And much the same prattle must be gone through all over again. ". . . delight to my old eyes . . . so very kind of you . . . very warm day; might I presume, sir, to offer you a seat outside?"

So Sherlock Holmes is hospitably settled on the shady porch, where breezes mitigate the heat, and Mrs. Lane is offering iced lemonade and macaroons, before Holmes succeeds in addressing business once more.

"Lane," he asks the venerable butler, "what exactly alarms you and Mrs. Lane about this package you recently received?"

Well trained by decades of sorting out household disorder, Lane answers methodically. "First and foremost, Mister Sherlock, the way it came in the middle of the night and we don't know who left it there."

For the first time looking less than bored, the great detective leans forward in his cushioned wicker chair. "Left it where?"

"At the kitchen door. We wouldn't have found it till morning if it were not for Reginald."

The shaggy collie dog, who is lying flat on his side nearby, raises his blunt head when he hears his name.

"We've been letting him sleep indoors," explains Mrs. Lane as she settles her amplitude in another chair, "being that he's getting along in years, like us."

Reginald lays his head down again and thumps his furry tail against the floor-boards of the porch.

"He barked, I suppose?" Sherlock Holmes is growing impatient.

"Oh, he barked like a tiger, he did!" Mrs. Lane nods emphatically. "But even so, I don't suppose we would have heard him if it were not that I've been sleeping in the library on the davenport, begging your pardon, Mister Sherlock, because the stairs plague my knees so."

"But I was in our proper quarters," says Lane with emphasis, "and knew nothing of the matter until Mrs. Lane summoned me with the bell."

"Leaping at the kitchen door and barking like a lion, he was!" Presumably Mrs. Lane refers to the dog. Her excited comments quite contrast with her husband's careful report, especially given that neither tigers nor lions bark. "I was afraid to do a thing until Mr. Lane came down."

Sherlock Holmes leans back in his chair with his aquiline features resuming their usual expression of disappointment with the folly of humankind. "So when you eventually investigated, you found a parcel, but no sign of the mysterious person or persons who had left it there at—what time was it?"

Lane answers, "Three-twenty of Thursday morning, or thereabouts, Mister Sherlock. I went and hunted a bit outside, but it was a dark night, cloudy like, and nothing to be seen."

"Of course. So you brought the package inside but you did not open it. Why not?"

"Not for us to presume, Mister Sherlock. Also the parcel itself is peculiar in several ways rather difficult to explain."

It appears that Lane is going to attempt to explain anyway, but Sherlock Holmes raises a commanding hand to stop him. "I will rely upon my own impressions. Kindly bring me this mysterious parcel."

Not so much a parcel as a flat, oversized envelope made of heavy brown paper glued together, it is so lightweight that there seems to be nothing inside it. The inscriptions upon it, however, cause even Sherlock Holmes to stare. Every inch of the envelope's face is covered with crude ornamentation done in black. All four sides of the rectangle are heavily bordered with lines that include zigzags, spirals, and serpentines, whilst diagonally across the corners, almond-and-circle designs peer like primitive eyes, heavily outlined.

"Give me the willies, they do," says Mrs. Lane of these, crossing herself.

"Very likely they are meant to do so. But who . . ." Sherlock Holmes lets the question die on his lips as he studies the other markings on the envelope: crude drawings of birds, snakes, arrows, the signs of the zodiac, stars, crescent-moons, and sunbursts fill every inch of the paper as if afraid to let anything else in — except a large circle centred upon the envelope. Forbiddingly bordered by rows of criss-cross lines, this space at first appears to be blank. But Sherlock Holmes, who has taken out his magnifying lens to study the envelope inch by inch, focusses upon this central area with an intensity remarkable even for him.

After several moments, he lays the magnifying lens down, apparently unaware that he has placed it upon the plate of macaroons, and sits with the envelope in his lap, staring at the oak woods of Ferndell in the distance.

Lane and Mrs. Lane glance at each other. Neither says a word. In the silence, Reginald Collie can be heard snoring.

Sherlock Holmes blinks, looks at the sleeping dog, and then turns to the butler and his wife. "Did either of you," he asks, "observe the pencil drawing?"

Oddly formal, even cautious, Lane responds, "Yes, sir, we did."

"My old eyes missed it entirely," says Mrs. Lane as if confessing to a sin, "until Mr. Lane showed it to me in the morning light. It's hard to see on the brown paper."

"I imagine it was much easier to see before someone put all this crude charcoal elaboration around it."

"Charcoal?" exclaim both butler and cook.

"Unmistakably. Upon close inspection one can see the granulation and the smears. Charcoal powder has almost obliterated the drawing, which was, I am sure, done first. And as for the drawing, what do you make of it?"

Lane and Mrs. Lane exchange an uneasy look before Lane answers, "A very lovely, delicate drawing of a flower—"

"A chrysanthemum," interjects Sherlock rather harshly.

"—amidst a wreath of greenery."

"Ivy," says Sherlock even more curtly. "Would either of you happen to recognise the style of the artist?"

Silence. Both Lanes look distinctly unhappy.

"Well," says Mrs. Lane finally, "it does remind me of . . ." But of what, she seems unable to utter.

"It's hardly our place to say, Mister Sherlock," pleads Lane.

"Oh, come." Sherlock's tone exhibits a highly volatile frame of mind. "Both of you know as well as I do that picture was pencilled by my mother."

He is speaking of Lady Eudoria Vernet Holmes,

who has been missing now for nearly a year, although no foul play is suspected; it appears that the elderly eccentric has simply run away.

And shortly after she ran away, so did her daughter, Sherlock's much younger sister, Enola Eudoria Hadassah Holmes, fourteen years of age.

A considerable pause ensues before Mrs. Lane asks timidly, "Mister Sherlock, do you ever hear anything of Lady Holmes or Miss Enola?"

"Ah." If the great detective feels an odd constellation of emotions upon hearing his sister's name, none of them show on his hawk-featured face. "Yes, I have encountered Enola several times in London, although never to my satisfaction."

"But she is well?"

"She is outrageously well. And at first, she appeared to be in cahoots with her mother, communicating via coded messages in the personal columns of the *Pall Mall Gazette*."

Mrs. Lane looks at Lane, who clears his throat before venturing, "You broke the code?"

"Several codes. Of course I broke them. That is, all except one, of which I can make nothing." This admission sharpens the great detective's tone. "I can, however, assert unequivocally that my mother's code name is Chrysanthemum, and my sister's code name is Ivy." With a pointing fingertip he taps the faint pencil drawing on the envelope in his lap.

Both Lane and Mrs. Lane gasp so sharply that Reginald Collie forsakes sleep, rising to stand on four white paws with his intelligent head on the alert, furry ears up and nose working.

"Reginald." Sherlock addresses the dog as seriously as if he were explaining a case to Watson. "For months there has been no word of any kind from Lady Holmes. Why, now, does it come in this form?" His slender fingers perform a muted drum-roll on the brown paper packet. "And what's inside of it?"

Lane offers, "Shall I fetch a letter-knife, sir?"

"No. I cannot open it." A gentleman would not dream of prying into someone else's mail. "It is intended for Enola." Sherlock Holmes pockets his magnifying lens and arises, on the alert rather like the dog at his side; he is all sleuth-hound catching a scent. "I shall take it back to London with me and deliver it to her."

Lane and Mrs. Lane, also on their feet, stare at him. The butler voices their doubt. "But Mister Sherlock, do you know how to find her?"

"Yes." With a keen glint in his eyes, the detective nearly smiles. "Yes, I believe I do."

CHAPTER
THE
FIRST

REPORTING TO WORK THAT FATEFUL MORNING AT my office (that is to say, the office of Dr. Leslie T. Ragostin, Scientific Perditorian, my fictitious employer), I wore a perfectly fitted princess-style dress of mistletoe-green faille, with wide organza collar and matching hat on my tasteful russet coif (wig), and, on the appropriate finger, a wedding band.

"Good morning, Mrs. Jacobson!" cried the boy-in-buttons as he held the door for me.

"Good morning, Joddy!" I smiled; indeed, I beamed; at last, after a month, the simple lad had it straight. Quite a contrast to the first morning I had reported for work in a seamstress-made dress (plum-coloured nainsook with filet-crochet trimming) and the ring.

"From now on you are to address me as Mrs.

Jacobson," I had quite firmly explained to "Dr. Ragostin's" assembled (and astonished) staff: Mrs. Fitzsimmons, the housekeeper; Mrs. Bailey, the cook; and Joddy. "Mrs. John Jacobson." I extended my left hand to display my wedding ring, obtained the night before at a pawn-shop.

"Criminy!" exclaimed Joddy, wide-eyed below the ridiculous hat required of page-boys. "Gold, hain't it? Real gold?"

"Um, congratulations," said Mrs. Fitzsimmons. "Forgive us for our surprise; we are quite taken aback."

Not nearly as much so as I was, although of course I could not explain how overnight, because my brother Sherlock had learned too much during the affair of Lord Whimbrel and the cryptic crinoline, I had been obliged to flee the East End, leaving behind all of Ivy Meshle's ready-made clothing, vulgar blond hair extensions, and cheap baubles, for I knew it would be necessary to change my identity.

"You have showed none of the usual, um, symptoms," elaborated Mrs. Fitzsimmons.

"Bosh," exploded the much more forthcoming cook, Mrs. Bailey. "This 'ere Mr. Jacobson, 'e lives right along wit' Dr. Ragostin, now, don't 'e?"

The other two gasped. This was the first time any of them had dared say such a thing to my face, hinting at the extent of my fictions, the white edifice of lies upon which was built my career. Certainly I ought to have squelched her most firmly, but she delighted and amused me, all puffed up like a hedgehog, so much that I burst into laughter.

The three of them gawked at me, as well they might. "Truly and bravely put, Mrs. Bailey," I crowed, still smiling even as I sobered. "Now, tell me, are you well paid here? Well treated? Is this a good place?" I inquired of each of them in turn with a look, brows lifted.

Each nodded fervidly, perhaps thinking of the exceedingly generous bonuses I had given out at Christmastime.

"Well, then," I asked, looking particularly at Mrs. Bailey this time, "what is my name?"

No doubt grateful in afterthought that her outburst had not seen her sacked, she replied like a co-conspirator, "Sure, and yer name is—is—blimey, I fergit."

"Mrs. John Jacobson." A commonplace name, so that my fictitious husband need not be the same John Jacobson known to anyone whom I might meet.

She actually bobbed me a curtsey. "Yes, ma'am, Mrs. Jacobson."

"Very good. Mrs. Fitzsimmons?"

"My 'eartiest good wishes, Mrs. Jacobson."

"Thank you." Not only my appearance had changed;

I was allowing myself a more aristocratic accent. "Joddy?"

"Um, just as you say, milady."

I sighed. Would the knuckle-headed boy never learn? "You must not call me lady! What is my name, now?"

"Um, Mrs. Jacobs?"

"Jacobson."

"Yes, milady. Mrs. Jacobson."

"Very well. Incidentally, I am no longer Dr. Ragostin's secretary; I am his assistant."

"Quite so, Mrs. Jacobson," they all agreed to my self-promotion.

"It will make no difference, really," I admitted. "Just go about your duties as before."

Without further ado they did so. I knew they would gossip with the other servants in the neighbourhood. Happily, it was a neighbourhood far from either Sherlock or Mycroft, and more happily, neither of my brothers kept servants. Still, I sighed with worry that some whisper might attract their unwanted attention.

But I worried less as June passed into July, the only remarkable event being that I actually ate well enough at my new lodging so that my face, and other parts of my personage, rounded out a bit, and I no longer required so much padding. I had taken an expensive room at the Professional Women's Club, where I was a member, and where no men were allowed on the premises under any circumstances; I felt safe there. This circumstance combined with the change in my appearance lulled me into a complacence that was soon to be tumbled onto its smug little posterior.

Not, however, before an interestingly confluent event commenced.

CHAPTER
THE
SECOND

UPON THE AFOREMENTIONED FATEFUL DAY WHEN I wore the mistletoe-green dress, no sooner had I arrived at Dr. Ragostin's office than the doorbell rang. And rang, and rang, and kept ringing worthy of a fire alarm. "Help! For the love of God, someone help me!" shouted a man's voice in tones aristocratic, melodramatic, indeed nearly operatic. Not in keeping with British restraint at all. "Make haste!" Did I not discern a foreign accent in his deep voice?

"For Heaven's sake, Joddy," I instructed that startled boy from my desk, "open the door."

As soon as he did so, I saw the shouting man, his contorted and flushed face ludicrously sandwiched between his shining top-hat and his starched collar, silk cravat, and city-coat. Striding into my office, making towards me as I stood to greet him, with apparent effort the fellow set his face in order. Quite a handsome young lord in a wild sort of way, he brought Brontë's Heathcliff to mind. "Is Dr. Ragostin in?" he demanded like one who has nearly lost his mind, but not his manners; he removed his hat, showing hair as black as a raven.

"Unfortunately not. Nor is he expected back for some time." My ladylike faille and organza quite showed me to be no mere servant, thereby starching my nerve. "As Dr. Ragostin's personal assistant, perhaps I can render you some assistance? Please be seated."

He dropped into a chair as if exhausted. Almost miraculously, considering his usual ineptitude, Joddy appeared with a carafe of ice water and glasses on a tray. I poured, and the man accepted his cold drink, no doubt in order to compose himself as well as to comfort his hoarse throat. Meanwhile, I resumed my place behind my desk.

"Your name, please," I requested, pencil and paper at the ready.

His eyebrows, black raven wings, stooped. "My wife, who happens to be the third daughter of the Earl of Chipley-on-Wye, has unaccountably vanished in the most peculiar circumstances, the police are nincompoops, and I have no time to waste on any more fol-de-rol. I would much prefer to speak with Dr. Ragostin directly."

"Of course. Nevertheless, I am fully authorised to undertake preliminary action in emergencies. Now, please, I must record the facts. Your name?"

He drew himself erect as a flag-pole in his chair. "I am Duque Luis Orlando del Campo of the Catalonian blood royal."

Ah! Pronounced "du-kay"; a *Spanish* duke! "I am delighted to be of service to Your Grace," I recited automatically. Like every British schoolchild, I had the ranks of peerage drilled into my head: King, Duke, Marquess, Earl, Baron; forms of address being Your Royal Highness, Your Grace, Lord, Lord, and Lord. For oddities such as emperors, counts, knights, younger sons, and the like, one consulted an etiquette book. "And what—"

"My Duquessa," he interrupted with even more importance, "is the exalted Lady Blanchefleur, world renowned for her fragile beauty, a delicate blossom upon a frail filament of womanhood."

"Indeed," I murmured, rather taken aback by this poetic description, even though his wife's name did mean "white flower" in French. "And it is Your Grace's misfortune that the Duquessa has gone missing?"

"She was most unaccountably abducted, or so we believe, whilst enjoying her daily walk with her ladies-in-waiting." His skin had now gone quite white beneath his black hair.

"The evil deed occurred at approximately what time?"

"About two o'clock yesterday afternoon."

Very likely he had been up all night, then; no wonder he seemed a bit wrought. "And where did this take place?"

"Whilst they were having a stroll around the Marylebone neighbourhood. Baker Street, I believe it was."

"Ah," I gabbled. "Um." Baker Street! Where my beloved and formidable brother Sherlock lodged, and where I might be put dangerously close to him whilst investigating this case. "Er. Baker Street. Quite. Where upon Baker Street, exactly?"

"At Dorsett Square—"

Oh, dear. Exceedingly close to Sherlock's flat.

"—where, it would appear, there is an Underground station." The Duque said the word *Underground* with the characteristic distaste of a gentleman, disdainful of this newfangled, dark, and noxious mode of travel, as only lower classes generally used London's cheapest form of transportation. Even though the locomotives stored their smoke in chambers behind the engines, releasing it only at ventilation shafts provided for that purpose, still, the Underground reeked of steamy, gaseous emissions, plus an overwhelming effulgence of unwashed humanity.

Did my brother Sherlock ever use the Underground? Not once in any of Dr. Watson's accounts had I read of the great detective's setting foot in the Underground station conveniently located half a block from his lodging.

"Please, Your Grace," I urged my aristocratic client, "tell me exactly what has happened."

"Most foolish and distressing." Duque Luis Orlando del Campo raised both kid-gloved hands in protest. "I cannot continue to parrot the tale like a schoolchild. I demand you to summon Dr. Ragostin!"

Let me spare you, gentle reader, the wheedling, soothing, glasses of water, and waste of time it took for me to extract a confused account from him. Suffice it to say that, for reasons that remained unclear, his wife, Her Grace the Duquessa, had descended into the nether regions of the Baker Street Underground. One of her ladies-in-waiting had the courage to accompany her. The other had remained at the top of the entry. Eventually the first lady-in-waiting had come running back up the stairs in great perturbation of mind; where was the Duquessa? Both had then gone down to search, but to no avail. The high-born beauty Blanchefleur del Campo had quite disappeared.

How very intriguing. "The police have undertaken a search, I suppose?"

He raised his fierce, despairing face. "Yes, they searched, but found no sign of her."

"Could she have exited by another egress?"

"I am assured that there is none. It is ridiculous to think that she might have wandered down the tracks."

Ridiculous indeed, for to do so was to keep company with rats and to risk being struck by a passing train. "Could she for some reason have stepped into a train carriage?"

"No trains passed through during the time when she went missing. Both ladies-in-waiting are quite adamant upon that point, and the Underground schedule bears them out."

"Yet had the Duquessa remained on the platform, or gone up the stairs, they would have seen her."

"Exactly! It is impossible. I am at my wits' end."

"Have you received a ransom demand?"

"Not yet. I daresay I will. Not only am I well-to-do, but her father, the Earl—quite wealthy—yet such a bizarre kidnapping is inconceivable; inconceivable! How was she carried away? Without being seen? When no one should have imagined she might enter such a place, as she went there due to the merest foolish whim?"

"What whim might that have been, Your Grace?"

"No one has yet explained it to my satisfaction. The Duquessa's ladies-in-waiting simply fly into hysterics when I question them, and the police inspector could get no sense out of them, either. The whole world has gone mad. I believe I shall go mad as well! I have called upon Mr. Sherlock Holmes—"

How my heart jumped.

"—but he has gone to some ridiculous place in the country and is expected to return today. Indeed . . ."

The distraught Duque Luis Orlando del Campo pulled a magnificent gold watch from his waistcoat and consulted it. "He should be waiting upon me at this moment. I must go." He rose. "Kindly tell Dr. Ragostin—"

"Your Grace, I am certain that the doctor," I interrupted, keeping my voice serene although my thoughts were racing, "will need to speak with your wife's ladies-in-waiting."

"Both are quite prostrated."

"Very naturally so. Yet they must be questioned, and surely, if they would not confide in you or the police inspector, they will not speak freely to a male stranger."

"True. Quite true," he muttered in a distracted manner, his wild eyes searching the room, then fixing upon me as if upon a revelation. "Perhaps it would be better if *you,* a woman, were to interrogate them? Would you be willing to do so?"

"Of course." I refrained from congratulating him for so cleverly hitting upon the solution that had been my scheme all along. "Your street address, Your Grace?"

CHAPTER
THE
THIRD

I BLINKED IN SURPRISE AT MY FIRST SIGHT OF
Duque Luis Orlando del Campo's residence on
Oakley Street, for it was of Moorish revival archi-
tecture, most unexpected, especially in this exclusive
neighbourhood near the Embankment. Almost anywhere in London one might expect to see Greek
revival, or Georgian, Italianate, French, Swiss, Bavarian, ad infinitum, and often regrettably combined—but hardly ever Moorish. The home, built of
yellow brick, eschewed tasteful ochre-olive-russet
tones in favour of vermilion trim and peacock-blue
roofing. Ruby and emerald stained glass sparkled
beneath pointed arches striped red and white. Oversized checkerboard-patterned tile decked the entry-
ways, and the bay windows, turrets, et cetera were
surmounted not by ordinary shingles but by bronze

domes, like something out of the *Arabian Nights*. Achieving the front door, plying a knocker in the shape of a grinning genie, I mentally prepared myself for almost anything. A butler in a turban, perhaps?

No. Quite an ordinary parlour-maid in a flowered morning-dress opened the door to let me in, extending the usual silver tray for Dr. Ragostin's card, upon which I had handwritten my new alias: Mrs. John Jacobson.

"Is Mr. Sherlock Holmes also in attendance?" I asked the parlour-maid.

"Not yet, madam. We expect him shortly."

Oh, dear. If Sherlock appeared, I would need to devise a way to vanish.

The parlour-maid took my card up to the ladies-in-waiting. Not personal-maids, mind you, or even companions, but ladies-in-waiting, no less. Hmm. This could be interesting, I mused as I waited in a fascinating arch-shaped entryway all carved in arabesques and honeycombed with niches. Nor did these display the usual Dresden, but instead, a collection of curious vessels, pottery or bronze, shaped like every conceivable animal: elephants, lions, storks, fighting cocks, dolphins, crocodiles, cats—no, I saw with a bit of a shock, the cats were real. House cats of a slender, decorative, Oriental description lounged amidst the curios or walked with insouciant balance along the curves of carved wood. The effect was so exotic that altogether, as the parlour-maid reappeared to escort me upstairs, I half expected to be led into a seraglio.

The boudoir did not disappoint me. Its walls, above ivory-hued wainscoting, were surfaced entirely in brilliantly colourful star-shaped tiles cleverly fitted together. Around the low vaults of the ceiling ran a border of fat, stylised spotted horses; on one section of the wall hung ivory-framed Persian miniatures; underfoot lay the most lush and elaborately patterned Turkey carpet, and altogether the effect was gratifyingly foreign.

However, the two ladies who received me were unmistakably strait-faced, thin-lipped, pale-eyed British aristocracy, most likely the younger daughters of viceroys or barons. One of the young ladies was introduced to me as Mary Hambleton, the other as Mary Thoroughcrumb. The former wore turquoise satin merveilleux shot in shades of copper-gold, and the latter peach-coloured chine Pompadour taffeta overlaid with rose mousseline, both elaborate enough to make me feel quite humble in my simple princess-cut faille, however tasteful. I had to wonder: If this was how the Duquessa's ladies-in-waiting dressed at home, then what in the name of riches might Blanchefleur herself wear for an outing?

I saved this question for later, however, as the two Marys sat down, waving me indifferently to a third chair. Despite their rich attire they seemed quite poor in spirits, their eyes swollen and red.

"This is a dreadfully upsetting time for us," said the Turquoise-Satin Mary once we had been provided with tea, the maid serving me last, and the exceedingly upright postures of both ladies-in-waiting giving me to know they were being exceptionally gracious in receiving me.

"We have already spoken with the police," added the Taffeta Mary resentfully. "What is it that your, ah, Doctor Ragostin wishes to know?"

Playing my part, I opened a little valise I had brought with me, took off my nankeen cotton summer gloves and tossed them in, produced a pad of foolscap paper, and sat with pencil poised. "He wonders, first, what errand took you and your noble mistress to Marylebone?"

"*Errand* is hardly the word," snapped Turquoise-Satin. "Our dear Blanchefleur needed no reason to go wherever she desired."

"Our dear Blanchefleur"? Not "our dear lady" or "our dear mistress"? It would seem that the Duquessa was on extraordinarily familiar terms with her ladies-in-waiting.

"Her Grace was—I mean, she is—" Faltering, the lady-in-waiting seemed hardly able to go on. "A restless spirit . . ."

"Young," put in the other Mary, although she was

hardly past twenty herself, "and adventuresome in a harmless way, and her protected life often seemed dreadfully dull to her, so if a whim might make her happy . . ."

Tears appeared in her rather close-set eyes. *They both seem genuinely fond of their mistress,* I noted mentally, with a degree of surprise.

"A whim," I prompted.

"Yes. She wished to explore all but the most undesirable sections of the city. Somewhere she had heard that one could tell the boroughs apart by the shapes of their street-lamps. . . ."

Quite true, and a matter of some fascination to myself as well, distinguishing one preposterously ornate lighting fixture from another. I began to feel a certain affinity for Duque Luis Orlando del Campo's youthful wife.

". . . And she liked to look at them, so most days we took the carriage one place or another, then walked about."

"Quite natural and interesting," I assured them. "Yesterday's outing led you to Baker Street? And the Underground station?"

"Yes, but of course none of us would *ever* ordinarily go down there." Heavens, no, not where one might catch a whiff of cigar smoke, ale, or kippered herrings. "We were merely walking past, but at the entryway hesitated the most pathetic old creature —"

"Snivelling and whimpering that she was lame with dropsy, she could not manage the steps, and she would miss her train. I am certain now that she was part of an evil scheme," interrupted the irrepressible Turquoise-Satin, "but of course at the time we suspected nothing of the sort, and dearest Blanchefleur—"

Both at once they directed their gazes past me, towards the far wall, so pointedly that, turning, I looked along with them at a life-sized portrait of an exquisitely lovely young woman, her fair-haired, fragile head, especially her sensitive, compassionate eyes, forming the most extraordinary contrast to her rich and heavy red velvet clothing profusely beaded with gold.

"Is that *she*?" I exclaimed involuntarily, for after meeting the Duque, somehow I had imagined his wife would be his exotic and tempestuous equal, even though I knew her to be the daughter of a British earl and his French wife.

"Yes, that is our dear mistress, and it scarcely does her justice," said Taffeta in greatly altered tones, soft to the point of adoration. "Hers is the face of an angel and the heart of a sweet, melancholy child. A kinder, gentler soul—"

"Never was," interrupted Satin, "a more patient, saintly lamb—" And much to my discomfiture, that haughty young woman began to weep.

"Now, now, there, there," said the other one to her. "How were we to know? And how could we have prevented it?"

Turning to me, she explained, "We feel to blame, yet it all happened so quickly and so naturally—"

"That toothless crone with bristles on her chin!" choked Satin between sobs.

"Cried out straight to our mistress," Taffeta went on, trying to imitate a Cockney accent, " 'Oh, yer blessed sweet Madonna come down to Earth, ye'll help a lame old woman, won't yer, now? Them steep stairs, wuz I to fall, 'twould be the end of me, but I can tell just lookin' into yer angel face'—"

"Enough," ordered the other in strangled tones.

"I don't remember any more anyway," retorted Mary-in-Taffeta, "for by that time, dear, impulsive Blanchefleur was already helping the old beggar down the steps, and we lost sight of her."

Although the ladies-in-waiting did not say so, I am sure they had stood dumbfounded on the pavement. To help them along, I asked, "What did this old woman look like?"

"Like a toad in the most hideous old splayed straw bonnet you can imagine," snapped Satin, recovering from her tears. "I told Mary, 'You go in after Blanchefleur, and I'll stay here to watch in case you miss her somehow.' "

I am sure there had been some wrangling on that

28

point also, which we did not discuss. Perhaps a few moments had passed before one of the maids-in-waiting had ventured down the stairs whilst the other had waited above.

"And I searched and searched, amongst the most disreputable and wretched loiterers, up and down the tracks to the full length of the platform, but she simply wasn't there! I even looked into a broom-closet beneath the metal stairs—"

"Which for my part I can swear she never ascended," snapped the other, "so you must have missed her somehow."

"But I looked *everywhere*!"

"And the old woman?" I asked before they could start quarrelling.

"Gone as if she had never existed! Quite vanished! Like our darling Blanchefleur."

Chapter
the
Fourth

IN THE FACE OF THEIR DISTRESS, IT SEEMED HEART-less to remain any longer. Putting away my notes, I had just stood up to take my leave when my ears caught the sound of a voice raised in ire downstairs. ". . . headlines in every newspaper, 'High-Society Beauty Abducted,' 'Shocking Disappearance of Earl's Daughter,' 'Castilian Noble's Bride Kidnapped' . . ."

An unmistakable voice.

My brother Sherlock!

". . . yet you say you have received *nothing* in the morning post?"

The reply, whilst inaudible, was evidently negative.

"My fear is that all of the hullabaloo in the press may have frightened them off." Sherlock certainly did sound wrought. "And until we receive a ransom demand, there is very little we can do."

I felt surprised to hear him say so, for I certainly had thought of things to do—but until he left the house, I needed to remain hidden in the boudoir. "Ah, um," I asked the two Marys-in-waiting, "could you describe to me Her Grace's attire on that fateful outing when last you saw her?"

They were pleased to do so in considerable detail. "Oh, she wore her new walking-gown from Redfern, with the very latest in Parisian sleeves!"

"Bouffant, you know," explained the other Mary condescendingly, as if I might not realise: As fullness disappeared from the rear of female attire, the most ludicrous puffery was swelling the shoulder and upper sleeve; it seemed that there must always be a bulge somewhere.

"In moire silk all the colours of a pigeon's throat, with a box-pleated front and a wide belt appliquéd in white beading with a truly stunning Art Nouveau design—"

Art Nouveau? Perhaps my face looked blank, for she then cried, "Wait a moment; I think we have a photograph!"

I observed as both of them searched dresser-drawers packed with quite exquisite unmentionables. One of a stack of crisply pressed handkerchiefs fell to the carpet; I picked it up, admiring its luxuriant Venetian lace edging and its closely embroidered scarlet monogram couched in gold: DdC.

"Duquessa del Campo?" I guessed, handing the handkerchief to the Taffeta Mary.

"Quite so. Where *is* that photograph?" complained Satin.

As I luckily happened to be on my feet whilst they searched, I took the liberty of idly wandering the room, observing its many luxuries: an exquisite fernery, well-filled bookshelves fronted with glass, enormous exotic vases displaying peacock feathers as if they were flowers, the most delightful inlaid rosewood writing-desk—

Upon the writing-desk lay a half-finished letter, written with blue ink on paper of excellent quality displaying the DdC monogram. This letter interested me exceedingly, although I took care to appear aimless as I ambled that way. I deduce a great deal about a person by his or her handwriting, and Blanchefleur's handwriting appeared extraordinary for its modesty, with no flourishes, each letter simply and carefully formed; indeed, only its small size saved it from looking childlike.

The content of the letter was also remarkable. I should perhaps explain that I am capable of reading and fully understanding a page at a glance, perhaps because when I was a child I undertook to read the entire *Encyclopaedia Britannica,* and so became very practised and quite speedy. Although I have perhaps not got it word for word, the lady's letter ran much as follows:

Dearest Mummy,

I hope this finds you well, and dearest Daddy also, and I trust that he does not suffer so much from his rheumatism in the warm summer weather. Thank you for sending your recipe for eels in mint sauce with vegetable marrows; I have explained it in detail to the cook, and we shall surely try it soon.

My biggest, indeed my only news is my new dress from Redfern, which my sweet husband, on the urging of Mary T. and Mary H., has ordered for me; it is lovely, of course, and you shall hear all about it in a page or two, I promise— but Mummy, they'll have me over in Paris being fitted by Worth next, and you of all people know how badly I feel about such extravagance. What good or useful thing have I ever done in my entire life that I should deserve to be so rich? I know that Daddy would tell me that we are well-to-do because God intended us to be that way, and that the poor are poor for the same reason or because they are lazy, but I cannot just let it go at that. I see the poor on the streets—here in London one cannot go out-of-doors without encountering the blind beggars, the crippled soldiers, the frizzy-haired women selling nosegays of flowers, the ragged Gypsy children—and I pity them so.

I give them pennies, and my ladies scold me, although of course they are good enough not to tell my husband—dear Luis, you know how extravagantly he reacts to every little thing, either roaring like a dragon or giving me kisses so loud they embarrass me. I had thought his ardours would decrease over the years, but it is not so, for all that I feel myself unworthy to be his wife, childless as I remain. Of course one must neither despair nor be ungrateful, but how a Redfern dress cures matters is beyond my comprehension.

Forgive me if I sound ungrateful. I scarcely know how to express the turmoil of emotion

Truly she did not know how to express what she felt, for the letter broke off there, to be completed later. And similarly I hardly knew how to feel, for I had expected Blanchefleur to be a coddled and contemptible aristocrat, yet certainly she showed conscience, making me wonder whether, if I were to meet her, I might like her.

"Ah! Here it is!" cried Satin Mary.

I hurried over, and she handed me a rather large casement photograph, which I opened.

CHAPTER
THE
FIFTH

THE DUQUESSA'S SLENDER FACE LOOKED LOST AND forlorn amidst the glory of her own full head of golden-auburn hair along with her alarmingly elaborate costume. Her plaintive eyes met mine over the most extremely ruffled silken collar imaginable, with a soft bow at the side rather than the front, and a matching bow at the opposite side of the—good heavens, what a Draconian belt. Gawking, I blurted, "I believe Her Grace has quite the smallest waist I have ever seen."

"Very possibly!" replied Taffeta with pride. "Since childhood, dear Blanchefleur has worn a spooned corset."

Heavens! A corset extending all the way from the upper limbs to the lower, with a "spoon" of solid steel to minimise any frontal protrusion below the bust. And since childhood! I could scarcely imagine her suffering. I myself wore a corset, necessarily, in order to conceal items such as my dagger, but I never tightened it, and even so, I could hardly wait to get the stiff thing off at the end of each day—

"And she has always done so continuously, even to sleep."

The Duquessa kept her corset on even to *sleep*? Such martyrdom to the tiny waist was expected of noble ladies, but still, how—how awful.

"Except of course during her confinements."

Confinements? "She has, um—?"

"Unfortunately, both ended in miscarriage."

Well, no wonder!

"Very disappointing, and quite as painful as child-birth, greatly endangering her ladyship's health."

Indeed so. Good heavens, the Duquessa, maimed by such excessive corseting, might well have died. I could not imagine her having a child, as seemed to be expected of her.

"It occurs to me," said Mary-in-Satin, taking the photograph back from me, "that Mr. Sherlock Holmes ought to see this. I thought I heard him downstairs a moment ago."

Oh, no. Pretending not to notice what she had said, I babbled, "Her Grace wore gloves, of course?"

"Oh, yes, white net."

"And with her ensemble, what did Her Grace

carry?" For a lady on parade always carried something, whether reticule, muff, fan, or—

"A parasol of white net with a ruffle of moire silk to match the dress," Taffeta replied. "And in her other hand, a handkerchief."

This surprised me slightly. Handkerchiefs were usually carried by unmarried young women, held by the centre, letting the corners form a fanlike expansion, the more readily to be dropped if a desirable male hove near.

"Blanchefleur needed it," added Satin in answer to my unspoken question, "in order to apply it occasionally to her nose, as she had a slight case of asthma. Has, I mean." Her tone had grown quite stiffly starched; she was upset with herself and offended with me. "I will see you out."

Thus, abruptly, the interview was over, but why did she not summon a maid to remove me?

"Come along." She swept towards the boudoir door with the casement photograph still clutched in her arms.

Oh, my unlucky stars, she wished to show the confounded thing to Mr. Sherlock Holmes. Herself. Indeed, she could not wait.

Ye gods, what was I to do? As I followed the haughty lady-in-waiting towards the stairs, my mind darted like a rat in a trap, for the consequences could be most severe if Sherlock were to notice me. Even as I tried to assure myself that he would not recognise me in my stylish and womanly gown and hat, still, he might ask who I was, and if he were told I was Dr. Ragostin's assistant—no, it would not *do*. This situation simply could not be allowed; he must remain unaware of my existence, and—

And as we reached the turning in the stairs, I saw with plummeting heart that there, in the middle of the arched entryway, stood the unmistakable tall form of my brother, taking leave of Duque Luis Orlando del Campo himself, no less.

". . . do hope you will be able to shed some light in the dreadful darkness fallen upon my family."

Sherlock listened with his hands clasped behind his back and his head bowed, giving the appearance of greatest attention and sympathy, even though he no doubt longed to retrieve his hat, gloves, and walking-stick from the hall-table so as to be on his way—

The spindly little hall-table, or hat-stand, stood near the bottom of the stairway, and opposite the door.

Almost before my mind had worked it out, my eyes had sought and my hands had caught what I needed. Two or three cats were perambulating up and down the banister. The largest, a lithe, lion-coloured specimen, I picked up with one hand under his belly, carrying him under my arm and letting my valise dangle from two fingers, meanwhile patting his rather serpentine head with my other hand so that he should make no outcry—yet.

The Satin Mary, rustling ahead of me at a great rate, intent on Sherlock Holmes, saw nothing of this, nor did she or anyone else see me loft the cat as we reached the ground floor.

Although kind to animals as a rule, I must admit that I lifted the poor kitty briefly by his tail in order to induce maximum indignation upon his part as I swung him and flung him (with, dare I say so myself, admirable accuracy) onto the hat-stand.

The diversion succeeded beyond my wildest hopes. Not only did the unfortunate feline screech like a dairymaid who has just been kicked by a cow, but as he landed, his claws slipped and scratched upon the waxed wood. He knocked my brother's top-hat, gloves, and stick to the floor, and the table itself fell over.

Or at least I heard quite a crash as all backs turned to me and I slipped out the door. I heard someone, probably the Duque, roar, "Abominable felines!" and something about how they were always and forever breaking things, but I can report no more. It is my misfortune that I can never fully enjoy such scenes as the above, as I am generally fleeing whilst they occur.

But one must not complain. Once away from the house and around the first street-corner, I felt comfortably sure that neither my brother nor anyone else was particularly thinking about me.

Concerning the fate of the young Duquessa, however, I felt not nearly so comfortable, knowing that she had gone missing *underground*.

Very few of the upper or indeed the middle classes realised to what extent London was really two cities, the one above and the one below. Early on, there had been many rivers flowing into the Thames. Covered over as the city grew, they had served as sewers until the great cholera epidemic, after which a new sewer system had been put in to carry waste out towards the ocean. Yet the old rivers remained. And then the underground *railway* had been put in! All of which required tunnels for workmen, too. The wonder was that the city could stand upon such a Swiss cheese of undermining. Surely, in such a muddle, there must be passageways that villains could use in order to kidnap a wealthy lady for ransom?

I needed to investigate the Baker Street Underground station.

CHAPTER
THE
SIXTH

I TOOK THE UNDERGROUND THITHER, OF COURSE. So, whilst the great detective was perhaps still on the doorstep of the Duque's Moorish town-house hailing a cab, I was already at Baker Street station, where I left my valise in the care of the station-master until I should call back for it.

One of the older stations with only a single stairway, the Baker Street Underground consisted mainly of metal and murkiness, the flickering gas fixtures of its vaulted rafters unable to disperse the gloom. Like the high iron rafters, everything was made of openwork metal—the railings, the stairs, even the walls of the station-master's cubicle—providing, it would seem, no place for any villain to hide. However, unsavoury persons loitered on the platform, and there were plentiful shadows, and also—most disturbing—the sheer *noise* of wooden and metal wheels rumbling over the cobbles of Dorsett Square above combined with the clop of horses' hooves made the station a thundering drum which I stood *inside*. Always before, upon entering a subway station, I had hurried across the platform, intent on my own business, climbed immediately onto my train, and departed, enduring commotion and acrid odours for the briefest possible period of time. But now, even without the roar of a locomotive, all around me sounded such echoing, reverberating, almost terrifying clamour that I realised no outcry would be heard. Indeed, a woman could be murdered in the shadows here and no one would be the wiser. Especially if all decent citizens were intent on catching a train.

Or—this seemed even more chillingly plausible— a woman could be somehow led, lured, or forced by a thug or two out of sight down the tracks in either direction.

Given that Duquessa Blanchefleur del Campo had not come back up the stairs, nor had she departed on any train, nor, blessedly, had her body been found—why, then the only way she could have departed the station was by the tracks.

Yet—could it be done? If a train were to come by, would one not be crushed against the walls of the tunnel? I felt distinctly alarmed by my own thoughts.

This modern metropolitan dungeon was not only chokingly dense and shadowy, but also dank and dripping. The tunnel was even darker, and I had no lantern. Still, that *must* be the way she had gone . . . confound my own daring, which might one day be the death of me. As a child, I had always been the kind to cross a river not by walking on the bridge, but by balancing atop its balustrade.

Rolling my eyes at myself, I knew what I had to do.

Left or right? Choosing a direction at random, I strode to the end of the platform, which stood quite six feet above the tracks. But, after glancing around to make sure that no one was watching, I swung myself down easily enough and started off in what I thought was a north-west direction, to my left, feeling my way along the wall as my eyes adjusted to the darkness. Rats scuttled off, squeaking; this I had expected, along with the cockroaches, the rubbish, and the stench and dank dripping down from cracks in roof and walls.

What I had not expected was to find a ragged man rooting in the trash.

Such was the gloom that I was nearly upon him before I noticed him, for his filth blended with that of his surroundings. And I had no time to prepare a greeting, monetary or otherwise, for he noticed me at the same time, and turned upon me with a bellow of rage.

"Wot you doin' 'ere!" Well might he ask, considering that laundered and starched ladies did not generally roam the tracks. Appropriate dress is just as important to the lower classes as it is to the upper ones. "The likes of you don't belong 'ere! This 'ere's *my* stake, see?"

Already retreating, I did see: He was a "tosher," lowest of the low amongst the "worthy poor." I had seen them emerge from the sewers, redolent of underground creatures, rotten fish, rubbish and offal and waste and slime of all kinds, for the sake of "finds" such as wood, metal, coins, or occasionally, eureka! a dead body that could be looted of its cash and clothing. For the sort of people who do murder knew their way around the underside of London, too.

"You keep out of it!" he bellowed after me as if himself contemplating homicide.

With no reason to think he might be hiding Lady Blanchefleur behind his grimy back, I meekly obliged, vanishing down the track, making my way back to the Baker Street station platform. There, I took a deep breath, considered a foray in the opposite direction, to the south and east, one can but try, faint heart ne'er won fair lady, et cetera—but common sense prevailed. I had found out what I wanted to know, namely that people survived the tunnels without being crushed by trains, as evidenced by the presence of the tosher. I needed shabby clothing, a lantern, a large stick, and a Cockney attitude before I again attempted to explore these underground passages in hopes of hypothesising where the Duquessa might have been taken. With my heart still thumping from the encounter with the hostile troll of the tracks, I reclaimed my valise from the station-master, then fled upstairs, glad to reach the light and air (comparatively speaking) of Dorsett Square, through the middle of which ran Baker Street.

Beer-wagons and bread-wagons, water-carriers, pony-carts, barouches, and broughams passed in constant, necessarily slow procession; an omnibus trundled by, advertising the inevitable "Nestlé's Milk." Many and various people also traversed the cobbles of the square: a fish-porter with a basket of fresh pollock on his head; a bill-sticker carrying his long brush and a bucket of paste, with a roll of advertisements under his arm; a ginger-cake seller; promenading ladies; businessmen in top-hats; laughing children (including some rather well-grown girls!) swinging from a rope they had tied to the top of a lamppost; and a hokey-pokey (that is to say, ice-cream) vendor who had set up his churn and folding table in the midst of everything, crying,

"Hokey-pokey, penny a lump!
That's the stuff to make you jump!"

Ha. The tosher had made me jump quite enough. Still, I wanted, indeed I considered that I deserved, some ice-cream, and strode in that direction—but suddenly and squarely in my way stood an old Gypsy woman almost as tall as I.

How annoying. Gypsy women in the city were beggars, wheedling for pennies whilst on their arms and ears and around their necks over their low-cut bright-coloured blouses they wore a weighty fortune in gold, solid gold beads and chains and bangles, all their worldly wealth on their bodies at all times, gleaming against their rough brown skin. And all over their garish garments are sewed circular tin and copper amulets that flash and dangle, "magical" talismans etched with depictions of birds, snakes, arrows, stars, sunbursts, crescent moons, and great staring eyes. I think it was because of the strong superstition they carried with them, the "evil eye," the Gypsy curse, that no one tried to steal their gold.

This Gypsy woman was dressed like the others. But instead of the usual whining plea, she addressed me in a deep, husky voice. "Child," she said, "I see a dagger riding in your bosom and a raven on your shoulder."

She astounded me so much that I stopped short,

for there *was*, as always, a dagger sheathed in the busk of my corset, and no earthly way she could have known this. Speechless, I stared at her standing there arrow-straight and lance-strong yet hollow-cheeked, with grey hair as long and coarse as a moorland horse's tail trailing down her shoulders.

Only later, on reflection, did I wonder whether she spoke of the dagger as an intangible quality, like the raven, ominous yet wise. Certainly no corporeal raven rode my shoulder.

In the same low, quiet way, she said, "You are in danger, cloaked in shadow, my child."

True enough, but there was no way she should have known it, nor was there any reason for her to call me "child" when I dressed as a woman grown.

My astonishment gave voice to irritation. "For all I know, you're the danger. What do you want?"

"I want to see the palm of your hand, child."

"And you want me to cross yours with silver, I daresay."

"No. Give me nothing. It is only that—that something about you—I recognise."

Simultaneously, weirdly so, I recognised something about *her*. Rather, something that she wore. Amidst the many circular amulets hanging all over her clothing, one stood out, for it was not crafted of copper or tin, but rather of wood, a thin circle of wood, and it was not moulded, but painted with a yellow design. To the casual glance of a stranger it might look like a sunburst, but to me it was unmistakably a chrysanthemum blossom.

Rendered in brushstrokes I knew the way one knows one's own handwriting, without reasoning.

Instantly, I confess, I forgot all thoughts of the unfortunate Duquessa, along with my manners. Without a word of explanation I lunged and grasped this talisman—the Gypsy woman wore it on the neck of her blouse, partly hidden by her hair and her many gold chains—and even though I had laid hands upon her without so much as a by-your-leave, she made no effort to prevent me, but stood like an iron signpost.

The wooden circlet—it appeared to be a section sawed from a branch or the trunk of a sapling—was sewed to the cloth through a single hole drilled at the top. With trembling fingers I turned it to look at the back side.

And there, yes, old habits persevere—there I saw the painted capitals, the initials by way of a signature. E.V.H., in dancing script I would have known anywhere. Eudoria Vernet Holmes.

Mum.

CHAPTER
THE
SEVENTH

DUMBFOUNDED ALMOST BEYOND SPEAKING, I whispered, "My mother painted this."

Although I spoke not so much to her as to the heavenly spheres and the firmament, the Gypsy woman gasped, as much astounded as she had at first astounded me. *"Your mother?"*

Her voice summoned me back to a semblance of civilised behaviour. I let go of the wooden amulet and stood straight to meet her eyes, which shone almost amber, like a cat's. "Yes, my mother painted that. There can be no mistake." And why, after all, should I be surprised when I knew quite well that for the past year Mum had been wandering with the Gypsies, Mum who hardly knew how to live without a paintbrush in her hand?

But the tall Gypsy woman reacted with reverence,

as if the noisy street were a hushed cathedral. Pulling a bright scarf up to wind it around the crown of her hair, she then placed her hands palm to palm, lowered her head to me, and said, "Blessings upon thee, O daughter of Mary of Flowers."

Such veneration, to which I was utterly unaccustomed, flustered me so badly I could not at first speak. "Thank you," I said finally, "but my mother's name is not Mary."

"She is a Mary to us, just the same." The strong old woman raised her eyes to fix me with the gaze of a seeress and spoke on in her low and softly rasping voice. "Long ago there were Mary of Magdala, Mary of Bethany, Black Mary, and Mary of Nazareth, who gave virgin birth. In our caravans we carry icons for them. But now has come a woman who speaks not our language yet travels with us, who saves us again and again from the wrath of police and gamekeepers, who makes the old icons new, who paints for us flowers for joy, flowers for sorrow, flowers for luck, so that we go where we wish and eat the fat fish and bow our heads to her and call her our Mary of Flowers."

"She is my mother," I repeated, "and I would like to find her, please. Where is she?"

"Where is she? Where is the arrow shot into the sky? Where is the treasure buried? Where does the owl fly in the moonless night? We are Gypsies, child.

We meet, we greet, we go again, wherever the wind blows."

She said these things not as if to make folly of my question but more as a litany. Yet I sensed evasion. Something she was not telling me.

I tried again. "With what caravan does she travel?"

"With the caravan of many beautiful horses, child, black starred with white. May I see your hand now? Often have I held your mother's hand, studied the lines of her palm, and told her fortune for no reason except that I revere her. There will be no crossing of my palm with silver. May I read your hand?"

Let the gentle reader please be assured that I took palmistry no more seriously than I did the making of wishes whilst blowing out birthday candles. I had been raised in an enlightened family, my father a logician, my mother a Suffragist, all of us free-thinkers who scorned superstition and regarded fortune-telling as a parlour amusement.

Yet I saw nothing to be gained by refusing the Gypsy woman her wish, whereas something might come of talking with her longer.

There we stood on the busy street, and paying no attention to horses, vehicles, or passersby, the Gypsy woman grasped both of my ungloved hands with surprising gentleness in her dry, tough fingers. She looked first at the backs of my hands, and then turning them, she studied the palms, squeezing my left hand with an odd unsmiling affection. "It might as well be your mother's all over again," she remarked, "except that it has a longer, deeper, and less divided line of the heart." She gave my left hand back to me. "That one belongs to the past and the family. It is the right hand that shows one's true self, both fate and deeds."

"Even if one is left-handed?" Like my parents I question everything, but also I remembered Cecily, the left-handed lady who became a slave to society's expectations when she was forced to use her right hand.

Fleetingly the Gypsy grimaced. "Such a question could come only from your mother's daughter. Are you left-handed?"

"No."

"Then why ask? Hush, child, and let me see. . . ." She studied the palm of my right hand with such fixed intensity that time seemed to recede along with the clamour of the city and the passing of traffic in the square. When she began to trace the features of my palm with the feather-light touch of a fingertip, I felt her touch reverberate throughout my person-age to my deepest being. I stood without moving because I chose to do so, but also as if in a sort of trance.

She said in the rhythmic tones of a Mesmerist, "Your line of destiny begins with a star on the mound of Saturn and runs strongly into your line of life. The wedding ring on your left hand tells a lie. In truth you are alone, you have been alone even in your childhood days, and you are fated to be alone all your life unless you act to defy your fate."

I felt the truth of the words settle heavily, like a brick, in my bosom, yet I merely nodded. "What else?"

"Your heart line, again on this hand, long and strong. You have a deeply loving nature, yet no lover. You address this problem by loving humankind. You try to help, to serve, to do good in whatever way you can."

Her manner was so matter-of-fact that no blushes were necessary; again I merely nodded.

She went on. "Your hand is slender and sensitive, of an artistic nature, and your sun line shows great intelligence and intuition. It begins with a star on the mound of Apollo. One star on a hand is rare. Two stars—never before have I seen this, not even on your mother's palm."

Instantly I had but one thought. "Where is my mother?"

"Your hand cannot tell me that."

"But you can?"

"I can speak only for the Mary of Magdala, the Mary of Bethany, the Black Mary. Your mother is where your mother is fated to be. You, Enola, must beware of following her. Follow your own stars. That is all I have to say to you. Now I go."

And there I stood for a moment like a statue with my right hand extended until I blinked as if awakening and looked around me. I had not told the Gypsy woman my name. How had she known my name?

Where was she?

I scanned Dorsett Square, and although my glance once more encountered the hokey-pokey man (with nary a thought of ice-cream this time), the girls swinging from the lamppost, and all the rest of it, I could not see the tall Gypsy woman anywhere. Where had she gone? Her disappearance seemed almost supernatural.

Nonsense, I told myself. She could have concealed herself in the public lavatory, for at Dorsett Square stood one of London's monuments to hygiene, featuring iron columns, carved Grecian figures, and a clock tower. Or she could have gone into the Underground. Or she could even have taken a cab, for directly in front of the Underground station was a cab-stand, of course. But this escape route seemed less likely. Because of the fine summertime weather, open-fronted hansom cabs were plentiful and four-wheeled "growlers," the sort of cab one could hide in, rather lacking.

To hide, however, was quite what I wanted, suddenly realising how badly my dress and person were stained and grimed by my venture into the tunnel, and even more so, how dishevelled were my thoughts and emotions. Hurrying back downstairs into the dim Underground, I took the first train, and by a circuitous route made my way to the Professional Women's Club. I needed to calm myself and think.

CHAPTER THE EIGHTH

MY ROOM, LIKE THE EXCLUSIVELY FEW OTHERS IN the third storey of this sanctuary, was rather Spartan in its furnishings; this was, after all, a haven for intellectual women interested in Dress Reform and other freedoms, not likely to care whether the tables were draped or the bed wore a skirt. But the food, as I have said, was excellent. I ordered a plate of sandwiches to be brought to my room, and then, once bathed, I sat in my dressing-gown devouring tuna-paste, cucumber, and watercress, attempting to comfort both body and mind. I reminded myself that today was not the first time I had encountered someone who knew my mother. I had overheard her Suffragist contemporaries speaking of her the first time I visited the club. I could not understand why my encounter with the Gypsy woman had left me so flummoxed, and as is my custom when such is the case, I turned to paper and pencil.

Swiftly I sketched picture after picture. I drew the Gypsy woman's face; the intensity of her catlike gaze almost frightened me. I drew a raven in flight, certainly not riding on my shoulder; in olden times, speaking ravens accompanied soothsayers, but also the black birds flocked to battlefields, waiting to feed on death. I drew the ill-tempered tosher in the Underground tunnel, caricaturing his strawberry nose and cauliflower ears as revenge for the scare he had given me. I tried to draw the Gypsy woman again but found her turning into Mum; this was most disconcerting, as I could not normally call my mother's features clearly to mind; seeing them emerge hurt my heart. Turning that sketch face-down, I tried another, drawing a delicate, lovely lady, fair-haired and slender, with the most exquisitely sensitive eyes. She soothed my feelings so that I was drawing her again from a different angle before I realised she was Blanchefleur, Duquessa del Campo.

Oh, for Heaven's sake, there I sat—I'd be drawing horsies next—eating fish-paste sandwiches, when I should be finding out what had happened to her!

Shoving all other thoughts aside along with my sketches, I set to work, attempting to reason out, on paper, what might have become of Lady Blanchefleur.

Either she disappeared of her own free will
  or she has met with accident or foul play.
If her own will, how did she hide from
  searching ladies-in-waiting?
Down track? Most unlikely, but must be
  investigated.
Must learn more about lady's background—
  unhappiness? Her letter to her mum not
  cheerful.
If accident or foul play?
Accident: She fell through a grating into
  a sewer, broke her leg so she cannot climb
  out, and no one can hear her screams?
  Unspeakably melodramatic.
Foul play: She has been taken by force.
For ransom—but no demand has been
  received.
For some other purpose? Revenge? Who
  is her enemy?

Again, inquire into lady's background. Perhaps the entire subway story is a fiction concocted by the ladies-in-waiting?

But surely the emotion I had observed in them was genuine. I did not believe that last sentence for a moment, and none of my other jottings felt particularly insightful, either.

In such cases one quite needs to cease thinking for an hour or two, thereby letting the mind alone to do its work. But how to distract myself meanwhile?

Visit Mrs. Tupper, of course! It had been several days, my dear deaf former landlady would be delighted to see me, and the venture was always quite a diversion. At once I arose from my chair to prepare.

Mrs. Tupper, I must explain, was now a guest-in-residence at the amazingly populous house of Florence Nightingale. Unfortunately, my brother Sherlock knew this, surely deduced that I visited her, and I believe kept watch for me. The street urchins I often saw hanging about might well have been his "Baker Street Irregulars." However, he would have described me to them as a studious or spinsterish female in tweed or some other drab, dark garb, with mud-brown hair yanked back in a bun and an alarming nose disguised by spectacles.

Such being the case, whenever I visited Mrs. Tupper, for the sake of my own safety I went as an exquisitely lovely lady.

I will spare the gentle reader the rigours of the facial emollients and tinctures necessary to effect this transformation, except to mention that as usual I affixed a small birthmark to my temple to draw attention away from the centre of my face, that is to say my proboscis, the prominence of which was further diminished by my full, luxurious (and quite expensive) chestnut-coloured wig.

But I cannot deny myself a description of the afternoon calling-costume I wore that day, a heavenly confection of cerulean blue dotted swiss gathered into scallops over a skirt of midnight blue, with a wide white satin belt, a blue bodice trimmed in white, a dainty blue hat topped with daisies and ribbons, and a blue-and-white parasol ruffled with dotted swiss. In fawn gloves and gaiters, I looked, if I do say it myself, rather a dream.

Indeed, I took a hansom cab to Mayfair so that I might enjoy, whilst pretending not to notice, the admiring glances of the populace. Never has a fair lady felt less presentiment of impending doom.

Alighting from my cab in front of Florence Nightingale's handsome brick house, I turned to pay the cabbie —

Nearby and closing in on me I heard the most astonishing, almost human cries of joy. The next moment, furry feet nearly bowled me over! As I turned to see what had jumped upon me, time played the most peculiar trick, rather like an accordion with all the air pumped out of it; I might as well have been a child again, so instantly I embraced my beloved dog.

"Reginald!" Without a thought for my dress, for appearances, onlookers, or anything else except Reginald Collie, I sat right down on the pavement to hug him in both arms, laughing and weeping as he waggled and licked my face and cried canine yawps of joy.

Bliss. For brief, ecstatic moments. Then a pair of long, slender, but strong hands came down, clipping a leash to Reginald's collar, and I looked up into the carefully expressionless face of my brother Sherlock.

But I refused to let go of my happiness. Still laughing, I extended a hand to him and let him help me to my feet. "Mr. Sherlock Holmes!" I burbled in dulcet tones an octave higher than my normal speaking voice. "Oh, just wait until I tell my aunt that I have met the famous Sherlock Holmes!"

Astonishment trumped control; his jaw fairly dropped for a moment before he disciplined it. "That was *you* in Watson's parlour?"

"Studying the bizarre bouquet his enemy had sent him. Yes." Still caressing Reginald with one hand, brushing dog hair from my dress with the other, I challenged Sherlock, "Now, confess, you would never have known me if it were not for our furry old friend here."

"I admit you are quite right. I am utterly taken aback. I do hope that the wedding ring I feel beneath your glove is merely part of your disguise?"

"Quite so."

"Then you remain unmarried and, it is fervidly to be hoped, virginal?"

"My dear brother!" I protested with some asperity.

"Forgive me. Of course I should not ask, but—I am all confusion—even I, seldom an admirer of the fair sex, can see that you are quite lovely."

I felt heat in my face, and could not speak, struggling not to smile with too much pride.

Sherlock went on, "It would appear that *finishing school* is unnecessary."

My expression must have changed, frozen, for he hastened to add, "I no longer have any intention of coercing you into such an establishment, my dear sister, I assure you. Miss Nightingale has enlightened me regarding the, ah, disadvantages of young ladies' *boarding schools*."

"How good of her. But has she enlightened Mycroft?" For my elder, and exceedingly stubborn, brother was the one who held legal power over me.

Sherlock's glance shifted sidewards, confirming my suspicion: I was not yet out of danger. I must get away. At the earliest opportunity.

The thought wrenched my heart, for I quite adored the stimulating company of my brother Sherlock.

In his most crisp tones he said, "My reason for finding you in this irritatingly simple manner—I should have thought of it a year ago!—has nothing to do with Mycroft."

"Something has happened?"

"Quite an odd something. There has been a most peculiar communication from our mother."

CHAPTER
THE
NINTH

MUM!

"Then she is *alive*?" I exclaimed, my thoughtless response revealing the fear I had scarcely acknowledged to myself: Because I had not heard from her in so many months, she might be no longer with us. Not that she had ever been with us, exactly. What had the Gypsy woman said about an arrow shot into the sky, an owl flying in the moonless night? Mum rode with the caravan of many beautiful horses, black starred with white. Might this have been a poetic way to say she had passed on, expired, crossed over—I detested the conventional euphemisms, yet found myself taking refuge in them—

My brother's face assumed the superior look of a logician. "Because you have not heard from her in several months, you have thought she might be deceased? My dear sister, I did not hear from her in *years*, yet remained assured she was very much alive."

"Yes, because you knew she was cadging money from Mycroft," I retorted a bit tartly, masking the tremulous feelings brought on by my paramount thought: how odd, my encounter with the Gypsy only a few hours ago . . . but I said nothing of this to Sherlock. It was not a matter he could investigate with deductive reasoning.

Instead, I demanded, "A peculiar communication? How so? Peculiar in what way?"

"I shall show you and let you draw your own conclusions." He turned as if expecting me to follow.

"At least tell me what does it *say*?" I cried.

"I cannot. I have not opened it. It is addressed to you."

I could have screamed, my impatience shot to such a fever heat. "Is this one of your callous schemes to ensnare me?"

"Enola!" As he looked over his shoulder at me, I glimpsed emotion in his face, quickly suppressed. "No, I wouldn't dare," he responded dryly. "But we ought to go sit down." He inclined his head towards Florence Nightingale's house, where the front door literally stood open, as if it were a public building, with reformers, government officials, and sundry other visitors coming and going at will, although the famous nursing reformer kept herself a strict recluse in the topmost storey. "Surely you can trust me so far."

The truth, to my dismay, was that I would have trusted him a great deal further.

So into the massive brick house on South Street we went, unannounced and utterly unnoticed; in no other upper-class residence in London, I am certain, would it have been possible for a tall man in a top-hat leading a scruffy dog and carrying a valise to simply walk in, especially when accompanied by a willowy young woman with her hat knocked askew and paw-prints all over her dainty dress. Because the ground floor was crowded—apparently there was a meeting taking place; I saw a great many red Salvation Army jackets—the three of us (counting Reginald Collie) made our way upstairs to the music-room, where Mrs. Tupper customarily spent her days lest someone play the piano—a great joy to her, as even her deaf ears could hear the music if she sat directly beside the instrument.

"Miss Meshle!" she cried the instant I entered. To her, I would always be "Miss Meshle," former boarder and recent rescuer, no matter how little I looked like that pseudonymous person. My disguises never deceived her, for she had seen them all. Tottering up from her rocking-chair, she hugged me around the waist, and I laid my cheek atop her starched white house-cap, which barely reached my shoulder.

Meanwhile Sherlock brought two other chairs over, and we all sat down. There was no need to make polite conversation to Mrs. Tupper; indeed, she directed all her attention to Reginald Collie, patting his head with both shaky hands and exclaiming, "Wot a darlin' good old-fashioned farm collie, the way a collie oughter be, not one of them needle-nosed spider-legged things ye see in Hyde Park . . ."

Meanwhile, Sherlock laid his valise across his knees, opened it, and withdrew from it a large, flat packet made of brown paper, which he passed to me. "Some unknown person left this at the kitchen door of Ferndell in the middle of the night."

Staring at the primitive charcoal renditions of stars, eyes, owls, arrows, snakes, moon, and sun, I told him with great certainty, "A Gypsy put it there." I had seen just such designs very recently on the amulets of a certain Gypsy. I had also seen such designs many times before, painted on their colourful wagons.

"A Gypsy! What makes you say so?"

"Why, she has been roaming with them ever since—" The expression on his face reminded me. "Oh, dear. I forgot you didn't know."

"How on earth do *you* know?"

"I guessed, and then I asked her in the newspaper. She replied in the affirmative."

"Would you be referring to that confounded nonsense about 'the fourth letter of true love'—"

"Forget-me-not," I explained. "The fourth letter is *G*. The flower for purity is the lily, fourth letter *Y*, for thoughts it is the pansy, first letter *P*, and so on."

He shook his head as if no less bewildered than before. "What would Mother want with a band of stinking, thieving Gypsies?"

"Freedom."

"But such wheedling beggars—"

"Bright caravans and beautiful horses, nights under the stars, no boundaries, the world's oldest nomadic people playing the world's most exquisite violin music, and no need to dress for dinner ever again."

"Stewed rabbit," he groaned, still shaking his head not so much in negation as inability to believe, "in a tin pot over a smoky, sooty fire . . ."

Paying no attention to him, I studied the brown paper, not so much the chrysanthemum and ivy at its centre—although the sight of that unmistakably familiar artwork squeezed my heart—but what puzzled me was the dark, ominous charcoal symbols all around, especially the four "evil eyes"—for that is what most folk would call them—in the corners. To me they seemed not so much frightening as frightened.

"Gypsies are superstitious folk," I remarked to Sherlock as casually as if I had not undergone the superstitious practise of palmistry with a yellow-eyed Gypsy a few hours before; I still did not know what to think of her. "These markings are just such lucky charms as they work into their copper amulets. But why have they scrawled them all over this packet?"

"If you would *open* it," he grumbled, "some reason might come to light."

"Wot's 'at?" exclaimed Mrs. Tupper as she noticed the package for the first time.

"We shall see." Although usually I open envelopes with my fingers, I thought I ought not tear this one. "I suppose I ought to use a knife."

CHAPTER
THE
TENTH

SHERLOCK STARTED FUMBLING IN HIS POCKETS FOR a pen-knife, but I simply drew my dagger from my bosom, from its sheath in the busk of my corset.

"Of course. How silly of me not to remember," said Sherlock in owlish tones.

Paying no attention, I slit the end of the thin parcel.

Pressing against its corners so that it opened rather like a mouth, I peered inside. I could see nothing except what seemed to be a muddle of shredded packing-paper. This I shook out, depositing it in my lap.

"Wot in 'eaven's name?" chirped Mrs. Tupper.

"Might you ever so kindly sheathe Excalibur, Enola?" Sherlock suggested mildly.

I did so, scarcely noticing his jesting name for my

dagger as I studied the mass of white paper in my lap. In a strip, or perhaps more than one strip, about an inch wide, it was partially covered on one side with blue-ink fragments of my mother's flyaway handwriting. I knew at once what it was.

But Sherlock said it first. "A skytale."

Such, I find to my astonishment as I write this, is the proper spelling of the word, evidently with its roots in Greek. I had always, since I was a child, thought of it as a "skitalley," for that is the way it is said. Mum and I had played at "skitalley" whilst I was learning to write. It was quite fun. One takes paper, cuts it into even strips, pastes them end to end, winds them around some cylindrical object, writes one's message lengthwise down the cylinder, then unwinds the paper. One's message, now all in bits and pieces on the long strip of paper, cannot be read by its recipient (Mum) until she finds the right size of cylinder to wind it around, whether broomstick, rolling-pin, brass bedpost, lamp-stand—possibilities at Ferndell were manifold but finite.

But what were the possibilities in London? Nearly infinite.

I would not be able to read Mum's letter until I had found a cylinder of the proper size to wind it round, and my frustration drove me so nearly to tears that I had to bite my lip. This was what I had been longing for since the day Mum went away: a letter, some words of explanation, perhaps affection, perhaps even—dare I think it—love. . . .

"I must contact Lane at once," declared Sherlock in decisive man-of-action tones, "to find out whether there were Gypsies in the vicinity the night this packet was surreptitiously delivered, and if there were, I must make haste to track them down—"

"Oh, nonsense," I cried with vehemence that surprised me, springing as it did from jealousy I had not yet acknowledged—but there it was; this was *my* packet and *I* ought to be the one to find Mum. "Mother has always taken quite good care of herself. Hadn't you better direct your energies towards finding the Duquessa del Campo?" I told him rather viciously.

He had started to rise to his feet, but mention of that name folded him back into his chair. He stared at me for several moments. "Pray do not tell me," he said finally, "that you came down the stairs and passed behind me in the Duque del Campo's foyer this morning whilst I was distracted by the most peculiar behaviour of a cat?"

"Certainly I will not tell you so," I replied sweetly. "I'll tell you only that Duquessa Blanchefleur is a lady who truly requires rescue, unless she has chosen a most unlikely way to leave of her own free will." I seized upon the opportunity to learn more about the missing person's background. "Have you contacted her mother and father? Or made inquiries regarding any discord between her and her husband?"

"Of course I have! By all accounts the Earl of Chipley-on-Wye and his Lady wife are scrupulously genteel and without pretensions. While quite naturally they approve of their daughter's exalted marriage, certainly they did not arrange it or force it. By all accounts, the Duque won his bride via old-fashioned courtship, has proved to be an exceptionally loving husband, and young Blanchefleur has every reason to consider herself a lucky woman."

His dismissive tone rather starched my spine as I thought of the letter I had seen upon Blanchefleur's desk, and her melancholy, her restlessness. Yet I had seen no signs of preparations to run away. Also, surely she would not choose to disappear in such an odd and uncomfortable manner.

Quelling my irritation, I spoke to my brother levelly enough. "I find it reasonable to think that her disappearance from the Baker Street Underground was not voluntary. Moreover, there can be only one way it was done: She must have been taken down the Underground track in one direction or the other."

"If her ladies-in-waiting are telling the truth."

"I am convinced that they are. You did not see their red eyes all puffed with weeping."

"And you did."

I refrained from answering.

"Are you suggesting that I should go search the tracks? The London Constabulary has already done so."

"And did they find no ways that toshers, tramps, and the like might use to make their way down to the Thames? Old river-beds, for instance?"

"Certainly they saw such rat-holes aplenty. To investigate each is impossible. If the lady was taken into captivity by such a route, there is nothing we can do except wait for a ransom demand."

"Nonsense. You can find the old woman who lured her into the Underground." A toothless toad of a crone with bristles on her chin and a flaring old-fashioned bonnet; why did I seem to recognise . . . But as my mind cast a flickering image like something from a magic lantern, my speech continued. "I do not think Duquessa Blanchefleur was kidnapped for ransom; if such were the case, then surely a demand would have been received by this time. There are other reasons that villains might seize her. The old woman might have been a procuress—"

"Enola!" He actually paled, so aghast was he to hear such a word from my lips.

And as I had only the vaguest idea what a procuress procured, or for what purpose, in the merest spirit of argument I plunged on. "Or she might have been taken for the sake of her clothing."

I suppose I ought to explain that there was a great trade in stolen clothing in the East End, and there had been a few shocking cases of upper-class children actually being abducted as they crossed the street to play with a neighbouring child, then turning up, bawling and mostly naked, in a very different area than that whence they came. For this reason, few such children were allowed upon the street without the accompaniment of a guardian-servant.

"For her *clothing*? The Duquessa is not a child!" To the contrary, I thought; she seemed quite child-like in many ways, but Sherlock laughed heartily. "Most far-fetched. However, had anything of the sort happened, she should have been home again within the day!"

I did not answer. Indeed I scarcely listened, for at that moment I remembered where I had seen — indeed, had known quite well for a few evil days — an old woman with a bristly chin and a hideous bonnet. Without a word I gathered the papers from my lap, jumped up, hugged Mrs. Tupper, gave Reginald Collie one last pat on the head, and, abandoning my gloves and parasol, ran towards the stairs.

"Enola!" I heard Sherlock shout in quite a wrought tone from behind me.

Stuffing the skitalley — I mean skytale — into my bosom, "I shall send word!" I called over my shoulder as I darted downstairs, out of the house, and ran

for all I was worth, hearing Sherlock's footfalls closing in behind me—but the instant I reached the
street, I whistled shrilly in a most unfeminine manner, and a passing cab pulled up short. I leapt in and
thumped the roof, signalling the cabbie to drive on.
As it was of course a hansom cab, I sat in full view
of my brother as it trotted away; indeed, I looked
over my shoulder to see him about twenty feet
behind me, breathing hard and looking fulminous.
He would be after me directly. I needed a hiding
place—but also I urgently needed to reach the East
End. Desperately I needed to disguise myself as I
had never disguised myself before.

CHAPTER THE ELEVENTH

"WHERE TO, MILADY?" INQUIRED THE CABBIE through the sliding panel in the roof. You see, the hansom cab, or more properly, *Hansom* with a capital *H*, having been invented by a Mr. Hansom some years ago, quite cleverly put the cabbie at the top and back of the vehicle, providing passengers with a view of their surroundings rather than a much less attractive study of the driver's posterior. Hence the open-air vehicle's popularity on pleasant days. Perched high above the ground, the hansom cab driver controlled the horse by reins passing through rings on top of the carriage, and as for the flaps that admitted fares and protected their legs, he operated them with a lever, and communicated with the passengers from on high. Indeed, I had never seen a hansom cab driver get up or down—

Oh. Oh, my brilliant stars!

Like most of my more daring—or harebrained—ideas, it all came to me within a moment. The driver had no sooner asked his question than I answered him. "To your stable."

"Beg pardon?" His voice went a bit squeaky.

"To wherever it may be that you house your horse and cab." I presented him with a pound note through the slot in the roof. "Do not fear, I shall make it worth your while."

Not until we reached the ubiquitous Serpentine Mews did the possible obstacles to my plan occur to me; if my man worked for one of the large cab companies, how could I expect to be successful, and how many more people would I need to bribe? I could not think; all seemed hopelessly muddled. I sensed the invisible weight of the Gypsy woman's raven on my shoulder, I had angered Sherlock again, the message from Mum riding in my bosom felt, in my mind, as if it were actually burning its way to my heart, yet everything else must wait until I had found the Duquessa del Campo.

Indeed, I felt guiltily fortunate that I had such an excellent excuse for procrastination, because even in this short length of time, my feelings about my mother's missive had changed. No longer on fire to read it at once, instead I wanted to wait awhile longer, to allow myself more time to hope that the message might contain some word of motherly feeling or affection towards me. Without quite allowing my mind to shape the thought into words, I sensed that this might be my last chance. I would be devastated if disappointed. Therefore I had become a bit cowardly, willing to put off the moment of truth.

Meanwhile, my cabbie passed through the Serpentine Mews, turned a couple of corners, and pulled into a small stable at the back of an exceedingly modest house.

"Good. You're independent, then?" I stated without preamble as I let myself out.

" 'At's right."

No overseer to interfere. How very fortuitous.

The man still sat on his high perch. "Come down, my good fellow," I told him. Recklessly I lifted both my hat and my wig from my head, tossing them aside onto a bale of straw. He quite gasped, but I was not to be distracted by his feelings. "How much do you usually earn in a day?"

Standing before me now, he opened and closed his mouth in a fishlike manner several times before he managed to say, "On a good day, three pounds."

"I will give you ten for today's use of your horse, your cab, and the loan of your hat and jacket." Although I had always vowed I would never dress as a male, I comforted myself by deciding that technically I was not doing so, in that I would not wear trousers.

My lower portion need never be seen; the driver's seat had little doors that closed it in like a bucket.

"Here you are." I placed a ten-pound note in the startled man's hand.

It was not that simple, of course. My cabbie required several minutes of persuasion, not financial—though I would gladly have given him more—but honest fellow that he was, he worried that I wanted his cab for nefarious purposes. I assured him over and over again that my intentions were neither immoral nor illegal, that I would be careful, and that I would have his horse and hansom safely back to him by nightfall.

My intentions, actually, were simply to feel blessedly certain that Sherlock Holmes, even with the aid of Reginald Collie, could no longer lay his hands on me as I performed a very necessary errand: journeying to the East End of London, where I hoped to find the toadlike old woman with a bristly chin who had lured the Duquessa del Campo into the Underground.

She was, I felt almost certain, Mrs. Culhane, of Culhane's Used Clothing.

It so happened that I was rather unpleasantly acquainted with this interesting person from an earlier adventure—indeed, from the train that had initially brought me to London. On which occasion she had worn a hideous bonnet—and although London might contain hundreds, perhaps thousands of ugly old women in old headgear that flared like fungi, how many of them dealt in used clothing? Moreover, I knew Mrs. Culhane's ruthlessness and daring, and felt instinctively certain that it was she who had waylaid the Duquessa del Campo. Although she could not have done the entire dastardly deed by herself, I knew the sort of friends she had, and felt sure a couple of thugs had waited for her in the Baker Street Underground station. Although I had not the sketchiest plan at this point of how to confront Mrs. Culhane, still, there was a great deal of earnest truth in my tone as I told the cabbie that I wanted to use his hansom for an errand of mercy.

He rolled his eyes but gave in. "It's a right fool I am, but very well then. If ye'll do this one thing. Set down me name and 'ouse number on a paper an' put it in the cab. So's it'll git back to me in case of mischance."

Willingly I complied, producing paper and pencil from my bosom to write down his name and address.

"Yer name, missus?" he asked.

A most fortunate reminder for me to yank off my wedding band and toss it into the hollow of my wig. As for the good man's question, rather giddily I replied, "Oh, merciful heavens, I can't even remember at the moment, I have so many."

And somehow this unguarded, if quite irregular,

response satisfied him concerning me. He shrugged, almost smiling. He waited discreetly as I grimed my face a bit by way of disguise, hid my hair, which was already secured atop my head, under his bowler-hat, and covered my bodice, which was luckily rather low-necked, with his jacket. He assisted me (I allowed the gentlemanly gesture, although I required no help) as I climbed up to the driver's seat and closed its doors to hide my skirt. He handed me the whip and the reins, led the horse out of the stable for me, said, "Take care," and then I was off, clattering down the streets of London.

CHAPTER
THE
TWELFTH

As I had only the most rudimentary notion of how to use the reins, I will admit that I felt a bit terrified atop the hansom cab. Certainly I am not afraid of heights, climbing trees for instance—but this high perch moved! Moreover, it moved in close proximity to many other large moving objects. I found myself jostling with vehicles of every description, carriages and carts, cabs and wagons, some light and fast, some heavy and slow, some going one way, some the other, trying to pass each other sometimes so closely that their wheels nearly scraped, or the shafts all but locked—sometimes they *do* lock, and then there is usually a ruckus if not a fist-fight.

Blessedly, I avoided such a fate. My cab-horse, appropriately named Brownie, knew his business, trotting along sedately and keeping me out of trouble.

"Cab!" shrilled strident female voices in unison from two of the most grandiosely begowned, bejewelled, massively bonneted, and great-bosomed dowagers ever seen upon a London avenue. Although startled to recognise them, I at once shook my head as if I were commissioned to pick up a fare elsewhere, trotting on. Once past them, in afterthought, I wished I had managed to splash some gutter-slop on them. They were Lady Cecily's termagant aunts, who with the connivance of Cecily's father had imprisoned and starved her, attempting a forced marriage! Cecily was now safe with her loving mother, and maybe someday I would encounter her again. The thought cheered me so that I smiled as I drove on, although I still did not know how I was going to accomplish what I needed to do today.

Somehow I had to enter Mrs. Culhane's shop and have a look about. If she were to recognise me, there could be the most unpleasant, even life-threatening, repercussions.

But I tucked the problem into the back of my mind as I trotted on, trusting my peculiar mental processes to deal with it along the way. As I reached the edge of London City and passed into the poorer district, the carts and baskets of street-vendors lined the narrow thoroughfares, sending up the most tempting aromas. Stopping my cab, I bought a meat-pie from a pie-man by pointing with my whip, flipping him twopence as he wrapped my luncheon in brown paper and hefted it up for me to catch. All around me workmen and urchins, shop-girls and washerwomen crowded the cobbles. Nearby, a beggar had attracted a crowd by exhibiting a tame tortoise that would stand on its hind legs for the sake of a treat, stretching higher and more erect until it fell over backwards upon its own shell, oscillating like a rocking-horse, to the great amusement of all.

Eating my meat pie and watching from on high, I laughed as hard as anyone, shaking my head in wonder as I threw a penny. One never knew what one was going to see on an East London street, whether ginger-cake sellers or a dancing bear, a woman hawking buttons and boot-laces or the most outrageous beggars. Why, back at the edge of the City, I had seen a beggar with matches who had brazenly positioned himself right next to a vendor of cigars, the reeking things. How males could possibly enjoy such an acrid "pleasure" was beyond my comprehension, although a few daring and notorious women —

Wait.

Actresses, mostly, but occasionally one saw —

Could I possibly?

Oh, my. If I were to try —

I thought I could manage it, especially if I tucked up my dotted swiss overskirt to hide it under my jacket.

Would my appearance then have the desired effect upon Mrs. Culhane?

Almost certainly.

Very well, I would do it!

Standing up in my high perch, I undertook the necessary manoeuvres to hide my dotted swiss, paying no attention to the exclamations and stares of a number of doubly astonished East Enders — not only was I, the cabbie, female, but partially disrobing in public! It didn't matter; none of these people would ever see me again.

After sitting down, concealed again, ignoring shouts, laughter, and a few catcalls, I addressed all my scant skill with the reins to turning the horse around. Then back I went to purchase a cigar and some matches. I lit the cigar, but wedged the stinking thing between the cab and its carriage-lamp to burn as I once again turned the ever-patient Brownie eastward.

By the time I reached the corner of Saint Tookings Lane and Kipple Street, the cigar had burned halfway down and extinguished itself, to my relief, for I had no idea how actually to *smoke* one, nor did I wish to learn. My purpose, rather, was to feign.

I stuck the cigar in the corner of my mouth, clenching its unburned end between my teeth with what I hoped was a most unpleasant grin.

Halting the cab in front of Mrs. Culhane's shop, I attracted the attention of a crowd of fishwives and street urchins, as hardly ever a cab came into this street. Their interest greatly increased as I got down. Gasps and murmurs arose as my skirt (now plain, dark blue) came into view. Although not common, and much disapproved for flouting the rules of feminine dress and appearance, "Billy" women were sometimes to be seen in London, generally with a bulldog on a leash. Lacking one of those, I glowered, brandishing my whip as I hitched the cab-horse to a lamppost. Then, with whip still in hand, I strode into Mrs. Culhane's shop.

There she was, her personage shaped rather like that of the beggar's turtle standing on its hind feet, her demeanour more similar to that of an outraged hedgehog. Although I took care not to look at her directly, I could see her chin bristles quivering, her stubby hands fumbling in the air, and I devoutly hoped that in her shock she would not see past my hat, my cigar, and my sneer to my actual face, or self, which she might recognise.

Striding past her as quickly as possible, I made for the back of the shop, raking its contents with my glance, and yes! Yes, prominently displayed was Duquessa Blanchefleur's silk moire dress with matching parasol, plus many luxurious petticoats *and* a long, expensively brocaded, spooned corset that might well have belonged to that same unfortunate lady.

But now what? Confound it, there was no way I could safely question Mrs. Culhane, and most unlikely that any information could be pried from her toothless mouth in any event. Better to leave the dress and parasol here until the police could see them, but I wanted something to prove my case. A handkerchief? Hadn't the two Marys said that their mistress carried a handkerchief?

I made for the basket where ladies' handkerchiefs lay in display, riffled through them, seized upon one I thought I recognised, and examined it.

Yes. In one corner, although the red-and-golden thread had been picked out, the impression of close stitching still plainly showed upon the fabric: DdC.

Duquessa del Campo.

Handkerchief in hand, defiantly tossing a shilling onto the shop floor, I exited.

It amused me, as I resumed my perch atop my cab, to glimpse Mrs. Culhane down on her hands and knees, hunting for the money as I drove away. Her greed was greater than her moral outrage, apparently.

Once around the next corner, gladly I tossed the cigar into the street and took a deep breath of relief, yet I suddenly felt bone-weary. Yes, I had got the handkerchief safely in the pocket of my borrowed jacket, and yes, it gave proof to my theory of what had happened to Duquessa Blanchefleur: Having been robbed of her clothing, she remained in the East End for some unknown reason—illness, prostration, lack of resources, restraint by some unknown villain?

So far, so good, but now what?

Wondering whether I should notify Scotland Yard or take my suspicions first to the Duque, I drove back towards the West End to return Brownie and the hansom cab to their owner. As I entered the City with its teeming traffic, soon my pace necessarily slowed to a walk, and then I found myself standing still, in a block-up that seemed likely to last for minutes. Setting the whip in its socket, sighing, just for something to do I pulled the Duquessa's handkerchief from my pocket.

And looking at it in the full light of day, rather than in Mrs. Culhane's dim shop, I saw something that had escaped my notice before.

It was perhaps the most disgusting good luck I'd ever experienced. Although she had taken care to remove the monogram, it would appear that Mrs.

Culhane had not troubled herself to launder the handkerchief, for in its centre, quite clearly one could see signs that it had been applied to someone's nose.

I recalled what one of the Marys-in-waiting had said about Duquessa Blanchefleur's asthma. Could it possibly be that I held in my grasp the nasal detritus of the missing noblewoman?

Although hardly a delicate notion, it seemed quite likely.

Even as I thrust the handkerchief back into my pocket in haste and distaste, nevertheless the thought struck me: Might the scent of the unfortunate Duquessa yet remain upon the handkerchief?

If so, might it (blessedly!) not be necessary for me to search the tracks of the Baker Street Underground, or other areas of London's nether cesspool? Perhaps not! Instead—I admit the idea occurred due to recent events instigated by Sherlock—might it be possible for a dog to track Blanchefleur from Her Grace's handkerchief?

Chapter
the
Thirteenth

THE IDEA OPENED MY EYES WIDE, STRAIGHTENED my spine, and so ardently surged my hope and excitement that they seemed to pass through the reins as if via telegraph lines. Apparently receiving a message, the good Brownie elevated his head, snorted, and plunged forward, forcing the cab through a space I would have thought too small for it! A moment later we detoured into a service-drive that led into a twisting maze of back courts and alleyways, from which we eventually emerged near Marylebone Garden. Invigorated, I sent the noble Brownie past an omnibus and straight down Baker Street, achieving a lovely trot—

"Cab!"

The imperious voice affected my heart so strangely that instantly I halted Brownie, although it would have been far safer to drive on. Senseless, reckless obedience! I dared not look at the man who had spoken, for he must not notice my face. But as I bent to pull the lever that opened the cab doors, I caught a glimpse of his tall, stork-like form, and those of his shorter, stockier companions, as they climbed in.

Sherlock Holmes, Mycroft Holmes, and Dr. Watson!

They all squeezed in somehow. I opened the sliding door on the roof of the hansom and said in the deepest, gruffest Cockney voice in my repertoire, " 'Alf fare more fer the extry weight."

"Agreed. Take us to Oakley Street," my brother replied.

Ah. Almost certainly they were going to see Duque Luis Orlando del Campo.

"Sir," I acknowledged in the same deep voice, sliding shut the opening above his head—but not quite. I hoped to eavesdrop.

But confound the din of the city in general, and in particular the rumble of my own cab's metal wheels upon the cobblestones, I could overhear nothing, except once when Sherlock raised his voice:

". . . an experiment, Mycroft, the merest experiment! I thought the old collie might be able to locate our daring and elusive sister. I had to go down to Ferndell anyway, for this."

"This," I concluded from their exclamations, was

the brown paper embellished with charcoal symbols. Apparently he did not wish to tell them that Reginald Collie had indeed found me, and that he, Sherlock, the great detective, had then lost me again, so he had diverted their attention by producing "this" from his valise. "Can either of you make anything of it?"

Watson's reply was unintelligible, but Mycroft's pompous tones struck my ear quite clearly as he excitedly lectured, "Why, my dear fellow, is it not obvious? You have your specialties, but you have not read as broadly in anthropology as I, or you would know: These borders and this encirclement are protective, intended to ward off evil. Something has frightened the sender, causing him to make these designs."

"And the eyes?"

"Very similar to the Egyptian Eye of Horus, or the Hindu Third Eye—"

"For goodness' sake, my dear man," Watson broke in, quite audible this time, "this is *England*, and the nineteenth century!"

"Yes, and still ladies promenade with the hems of their skirts and sleeves bordered with fol-de-rol that has no practical purpose—"

"Decorative!"

"—except that, since aboriginal times, all openings in a garment needed to be barricaded with magical symbols to prevent the entry of evil spirits!" Mycroft then evidently turned on Sherlock, for he demanded, "Who sent you this?"

But my brother's reply was muted, and strain my ears as I might, I could not tell what he said about Ferndell, or Mum, or me, except that Mycroft once roared, "The extraordinary nerve of the girl!" Yes, the nerve indeed, I thought wryly. He and Sherlock had no idea how nervous I was. Indeed, my nerve was stretched to the breaking point over the crowns of their top-hats as Brownie trotted on valiantly with his heavily loaded cab.

The nearer to the Embankment, the worse the noise, and the denser the traffic, until, reaching the Strand, my cab was barely able to crawl along. As my fare made no complaint, I made no attempt to force a way through the crush, but walked the horse until, near Charing Cross station, we halted, for it seemed that every vehicle in London had come together there. All rumble of wheels had temporarily abated, and though there was still a good deal of commotion—such as some wagon-drivers ahead of me cursing one another—still, I took the chance to try to hear once again what was going on inside my hansom, inching the opening on the roof a bit more widely ajar.

". . . why on Earth no ransom note?"

Ah. Now they spoke of the missing Duquessa, and Watson had resumed his usual puzzled tone.

"Many possible reasons," replied my brother Sherlock crisply, "but none of them hopeful. For instance, assuming that she *was* kidnapped for money, her captors simply lost their nerve and, fearing that she would set the police on them, dispatched her."

"My dear Holmes! Surely—"

"Alas, nothing is sure. Indeed, they might have taken her—the presence of the old woman suggests a procuress. If she was taken for the upper-class trade in the world's oldest profession—"

"A fate worse than death!" declared Mycroft.

"Quite."

Watson protested, "But surely all conjecture need not be so grim. Is there not a possibility . . ." The good doctor hesitated.

"Ah, you are thinking of my own peculiar family situation," Sherlock guessed whimsically, and apparently, rightly. "You hypothesise that the lady may have run away of her own free will?"

Sounding a bit red-faced, Watson mumbled, "Well, surely it is a possibility."

"Possible, yes, but not probable."

"Any woman might well wish to escape such an explosively melodramatic husband—"

"Ever the stoic British soldier, Watson," interrupted Sherlock with amusement, "to find fault with a perfectly presentable and quite wealthy foreigner."

"Well, the wife is British, is she not?"

"And French," put in Mycroft, "on her mother's side."

"Very well," persisted poor Watson, "partly French, and young, and very possibly unhappy with an older husband—"

"Watson, whatever their circumstances, women simply do *not* run off on a regular basis." Sherlock was beginning to sound a bit peevish. "With only two unfortunate exceptions that I know of—"

In tones of sincere apology Watson cried, "Certainly I would not allude to your personal misfortune—"

Something cleared out of the way far ahead, traffic began to move again, I trailed the tip of my whip over Brownie's back to signal him to walk, and after that I heard no more until I actually turned into Oakley Street and stopped the cab, remembering just in time that, in my guise as cab-driver, I did not know the exact address. I opened the door in the roof, my brother's hand shot up to give me a generous fare and waved dismissively to indicate that he did not expect change, and he, Mycroft, and Watson pushed the hansom doors open before I had put the money away. Just as well, as I had forgotten to ply the lever.

"What course of action will you advise for the duke?" Watson was asking as they got out.

"Duque," Sherlock corrected him with a hint of a sneer; Watson was not after all alone in his prejudice against the foreigner. "Well, perhaps I shall suggest that his wife ran away upon the Underground and is living with my sister."

"Come, now, Holmes. Are you truly so at a loss?"

"My informants tell me nothing. Thread after thread of conjecture leads me nowhere. I should never have taken the case," Holmes said bitterly as they walked towards the startlingly Moorish house a small distance up the street. "Missing persons are my Achilles' heel, apparently."

"Nonsense. A dozen times you have come within inches of finding your sister."

Make that a dozen plus one, I thought as I turned the cab around and drove away, my heart aching — I admit it; the mere sound of my brother's voice moved me nearly to tears, especially as he spoke so bitterly of me.

But it was not to be helped. And I had work to do.

CHAPTER
THE
FOURTEENTH

AFTER RETURNING BROWNIE TO HIS HUMBLE stable and the cabbie's jacket and derby to their proper owner—thanking the man effusively and sincerely—I restored myself as best I could to my former dotted-swissness, complete with hat and wig. Pocketing my ring (not that it mattered if I lost it; I had several spare wedding bands on hand), I made my way back to my lodging for a wash and a change of clothing, feeling myself much sullied by pawprints of dog and odour of horse.

Also, I needed dinner before I could act on my plan to find the Duquessa, and—

And the first thing I encountered upon unbuttoning my much-abused dress was a mass of paper cut and pasted into strips.

Mum's message.

Oh, dear.

Much as I would have liked to put it off, I knew I would not be able to face Sherlock again until I had dealt with the skytale. And I needed to face Sherlock in order to enlist the services of Reginald Collie. This very evening, if possible.

Standing in my petticoats whilst waiting for the girl to bring up hot water for my ablutions, I straightened out the strips of paper—there were no less than four of them, and all rather long—then laid them on my bed and peered at them, trying to think. Mum had wrapped them around some cylinder to write them, and no doubt she had supposed that the same type and size of cylinder would be available to me. But what could it be, when she was with the Gypsies and I was in London?

Nothing small, surely, given the width of the papers. Not a paintbrush handle, although Mum was quite the artist.

What else did Mum like to do? Look for wild-flowers, wander the countryside—a walking-staff? But surely she could not expect me to have one of those in London—

Ah! What *would* she expect me to have that she also had? I must think with Mum's point of view.

No small task, as I had never fully understood my mother. But I tried. What had Mum and I done together? Read books? Yes, indeed, but no cylindrical books came to mind. Gathered flowers and arranged them? Surely, but the vases were of various sizes and shapes. Other such activities, such as putting together baskets and birdcages out of sticks? Not Mum. No homebody, she. Much preferring to be out-of-doors, she had made sure I was provided with a swing, she had encouraged me to climb trees, she had taught me to ride a bicycle —

The girl chose that moment to knock and enter with the requisite ewer of steaming water, interrupting my thoughts.

After my wash, I experimented with wrapping one section of the skytale around the stem of a floor-lamp, shifting the paper this way and that, to no avail. Then I tried my reading-lamp, and then one of the railings along the stairway, with no better results. I could not even tell whether I needed larger cylinders or smaller. Most frustrating.

I went to see Sherlock after dinner, and in order to tweak his ever-so-superior nose, I wore exactly the same costume I had worn the day he had failed to recognise me face-to-face in Mrs. Watson's parlour. No gold ring, as I was being Miss Viola Everseau. From my polished button-top boots and my modest but lovely primrose-yellow frock to my rice-powdered face with its little birthmark, my carefully coiffed wig, and my Gypsy bonnet—how ironic, but that is what they are called, the flat little straw hats with a sprig of flowers—in every particular I was his sister disguised simply by being beautiful.

Rather petty of me, but like my brother, I quite liked a moment of triumph. In a carpet-bag I carried other clothing more suitable for the night's work that lay ahead of us. That is to say, I quite hoped he would come along. If not, then the night's work lay ahead of me, singularly Enola, as usual.

If Sherlock were not at home, I had decided, I would wait. But even though the sun had not yet set this long July evening, I rather expected he would be in his lodging recovering from a tiring and frustrating day.

Mrs. Hudson, answering the door, affirmed that he was at home. I sent my card up on a silver tray:

Miss Viola Everseau

Shortly I heard his rather explosive vocal reaction. Evidently Mrs. Watson, on the occasion of our previous meeting in her parlour, had told him my name, and he remembered it.

A moment later, joyously barking, Reginald Collie came bounding downstairs to greet me. Just in time, before he could leap upon me, I caught the dog by his front paws. "You are not to ruin *this* dress," I told him affectionately, "or at least not until Sherlock has had a chance to see it."

"I see it," said a terse voice from the top of the stairs, and as if my personal pulchritude bore no further discussion, my brother changed the subject. "Have you yet read our mother's message?"

Climbing the stairs to meet him, trying not to smile too broadly, I waited until I reached his level to speak. Then I said, "I have attempted to do so without success. But never mind that for now; there is more urgent business at hand."

"What could be—"

"I have discovered what happened to the Duquessa del Campo, and I know where we might find her."

His eyebrows reacted, to the news I thought, until he said, "We?"

"Reginald and I, actually. But certainly you may come along if you like."

Sherlock took a deep breath and let it out before he spoke. "I shall let that pass. And I admit that, whilst I have quite mastered my studies of the criminal mind, I struggle continually for the slightest comprehension of *yours*. Here you are as bold as brass, yet—why did you run from me so precipitously earlier today?"

"Surely it is obvious. Because I had urgent business elsewhere, and I knew you would desire to detain me."

"Indeed." After perusing me for a moment as if I were a specimen, he said, "I have quite changed my mind, Enola, about your future. I pity any man who ever marries you. Indeed, I think perhaps you ought not to marry."

An odd tangent, I thought, but it did not disturb me, for I quite agreed with him.

"Come in, come in!" he added impatiently, waving me into his lodging and tossing some newspapers aside to offer me a seat.

"I would like to study at university, actually," I confided whilst daintily I arranged my skirt around me and Reginald lay down at my feet. "The Renaissance, the German classics, Logic, Argumentation . . ."

With a pained look as if he were developing a headache, my brother interrupted. "You promised news of the Duquessa del Campo."

"Quite. I have been on the trail of the hag who lured her into the Underground. Although there are perhaps hundreds of bulbous women with bristly chins and ugly bonnets in London, I happen to know of a particularly unsavoury one, and I focussed my attention on her." Concisely, without divulging the means by which I had gone there, I told my brother about my visit to Mrs. Culhane's shop and what I had found: Blanchefleur's gown, her parasol, her petticoats.

"You are quite sure they were the Duquessa's?"

Only a man could have asked such a silly question. Or perhaps I should say only a gentleman, because males of the upper classes, dressing alike as they all do—even now, in the comfortable disarray of his lodging, I found my brother uniformed in city attire complete with charcoal waistcoat, black jacket, impeccably starched white cuffs and collar—resembling so many penguins, perhaps men of Sherlock's class find it impossible to tell one black frock-coat from another.

Therefore I answered gently. "My dear brother, dresses are as distinctive to me as cigar ashes are to you. I am completely certain."

"Could you not bring something away as proof?"

"I could, and I did." From my bosom I produced the fine linen handkerchief edged with Venetian lace, handing it to him. "I saw several just like this in Lady Blanchefleur's boudoir. You will notice where her monogram has been picked out."

"Quite. DdC. Duquessa del Campo." Evidently struggling to adjust his thinking on the matter, he muttered, "It appears . . . however unlikely . . . but why on Earth would the villains choose this particular lady amongst all the overdressed women in London?"

The answer sprang from me before I realised I knew it. "For the sake of her exceptionally long and luxuriant golden-auburn hair."

My brother stared at me as if I were speaking Swahili, but a chill in my bones assured me I was right. The villains had not only taken Blanchefleur's clothing, but also shorn her head, very likely doubling their profits.

"You have bought wigs," I said to Sherlock. "You know how expensive they are. I shudder to tell you what I paid for the one I wear, for the hair must be imported from Bavarian peasant girls who wear head-kerchiefs, or else be taken from female convicts, few of whom seem likely to have very lovely tresses, or sold by women so desperate they agree to part with their crowning glory—"

"In short," Sherlock cut in, "attractive hair for wigs—"

"And hair-extensions and the like," I put in.

"—is hard to come by and fetches a handsome price."

"Quite."

"I suppose you may be right," he admitted without enthusiasm. "So, hypothesising that this Mrs. Culhane and some accomplices seized the Lady Blanchefleur for the sake of her apparel plus her hair—is this shop in a very bad neighbourhood?"

"Rather."

"Some further assault or injury might have made it impossible for her to return home?"

"Such would seem to be the case."

He sprang from his chair, pacing, the man of action. "We must arouse the constabulary at once."

"My plan," I said rather loudly, "is to have Reginald Collie attempt to track her from the scent on her handkerchief."

At the mention of his name, the aged dog rose to his feet and deployed his ears.

I went on, "You have perhaps noticed that the Duquessa left some nasal, ah, effulgence upon the cloth."

"Yes, but my dear sister, Reginald is a *collie*, not a bloodhound!"

Reginald's liquid brown-eyed gaze shifted from me to my brother and back again as he followed the argument.

"True," I admitted, but immediately a better thought came to me. "What about that dog you used to track the Solomon Islander, then? The dog you got from the old fellow who keeps badgers and stoats and so forth?"

Sherlock halted to peer at me in evident shock. "You have been reading Watson's infernally melodramatic accounts of my affairs?"

"Of course, if you consider *The Sign of the Four*

infernally melodramatic. I believe the dog's name was Toby."

"Indeed it was. And still is." Staring down upon me in a most peculiar manner, Sherlock asked an absurdly irrelevant question. "Enola, were you serious when you mentioned a desire to go to university?"

"I—my classical education is good, but I have dreamt of learning higher mathematics, modern literature, sciences such as chemistry—"

Sherlock raised both hands in quite a decisive gesture rather like that of an orchestra director commanding silence before the symphony. "We will go immediately to fetch Toby, and I will come with you wherever you lead me, on one condition: Mycroft also shall accompany us."

CHAPTER
THE
FIFTEENTH

NOTHING COULD HAVE SURPRISED ME MORE OR pleased me less. Levitated from my seat by shock, I stood aghast. "Mycroft! But why?"

"There is not time to explain, Enola." Sherlock seized his top-hat, kid-gloves, and stick. "Do you agree?"

"How can I? He has the legal right to force me—"

"I give you my word of honour as a gentleman that I shall prevent him from attempting to capture or coerce you in any way."

"You will not let him lay hands on me?"

"I promise you, I will not."

Sherlock's word was inviolate. Also, I knew that I could easily outrun Mycroft should anything go amiss. But still . . . "I have a niggling feeling," I told Sherlock, "that this is one of your tricks."

"So it is." The corners of his mouth twitched in a puckish smile most incongruous on his distinguished face. "On Mycroft."

"Oh!" This information, of course, made it perfectly all right, and my curiosity utterly trumped my caution. "Very well, then!" I rubbed Reginald Collie's head good-bye. "Let us go at once."

Toby, just as Watson had described him, was a spaniel of sorts, with long brown-and-white hair but nothing else to recommend him by way of beauty. We left the dog in the cab (Sherlock had ordered a four-wheeler; what Sherlock wanted, Sherlock got), which waited for us whilst we went into Mycroft's club to fetch him. At this twilight time of day, it seemed, Mycroft was quite certainly in his club. He varied no more from his orbit to work, club, and lodgings than the sun varied in its rising and setting.

As a female, even as the lovely Viola Everseau in a delicately yellow gown, necessarily I waited in the antechamber, and Sherlock waited with me whilst a senior servant (as this might be no small task) went in to fetch Mycroft. Several minutes passed before that scowling individual appeared. Meanwhile, Sherlock produced my card from his shirt-pocket and passed it back to me. "Play your part, Miss Viola Everseau."

Oho. Sherlock wanted to see how long it would

take for Mycroft to recognise me. I held my carpet-bag in front of me with both gloved hands, tilted my head downward, and settled my face in a simpering expression.

When Mycroft burst forth, resplendent in white tie, expansive royal blue waistcoat, and cutaway jacket, he did not even glance at me. "Sherlock," he barked, irate, "you know I despise being disturbed at my—"

"Quite necessary, I assure you, dear brother," Sherlock interrupted in tones so suave that they smothered Mycroft's ire like sugar icing poured onto a hot cinnamon-bun. "Mycroft Holmes, allow me to present Miss Viola Everseau."

Mycroft turned to me with the scantest of bows, and I handed him my card. "Very pleased, I'm sure," he said, sounding not pleased at all.

"Miss Everseau requires my assistance," said Sherlock, "and that of another able-bodied man. As Watson is unavailable, I came to you."

"Able-bodied!" Mycroft roared as if he had been insulted.

"Oh, please, Mr. Holmes," I warbled to Mycroft in my most dulcet soprano, "surely you cannot refuse to assist a lady in distress?"

His mouth opened, but no reply was forthcoming. Rather, he looked as if he had eaten something that disagreed with him.

"Come, come, Mycroft," chided Sherlock. "It will be for only a few hours, and I have a cab waiting."

Hearing his cue, the astute servant appeared with Mycroft's capacious coat and slipped it onto him. (One perhaps ought to explain that proper dress knows no season. Even in the heat of summer a gentleman in evening-dress will wear his coat, just as a gentlewoman must wear her bonnet and gloves.) Sherlock took Mycroft's hat, et cetera, for him, immediately manoeuvring his stately brother out the door whilst I slipped out likewise. "Where to, Miss Everseau?" he asked me as we neared the cab.

"Kipple Street at Saint Tookings Lane," I murmured as if I myself were incapable of calling out our destination to the cabbie.

Sherlock did so.

"The East End? With a *dog* yet?" Mycroft complained, already in the cab, taking care to seat himself in the opposite corner from Toby. Meanwhile, Sherlock gave me his hand and helped me up the step as carefully as if I were made of Waterford crystal. Feigning a ladylike repugnance towards poor Toby, I sat next to Mycroft, where he would be sure to whiff my expensive lily-and-lavender scent. Sherlock lounged on the opposite seat, stroking the dog and saying nothing, as the cab rolled off with no more than the usual degree of jostling.

The silence lasted for some time, until seemingly

111

either curiosity, nerves, or my perfume got the better of Mycroft. He swung his impressive head towards me. "What, may I ask, is the nature of your difficulty, Miss, ah . . ."

I merely ducked my head and smiled.

"Everseau," volunteered Sherlock from the opposite seat. "Miss Viola Everseau, whose parents were great friends of our mum."

"Which reminds me!" Mycroft leaned across the cab towards his brother. "Have you heard from Enola regarding that communication of which you told me?"

"Not yet."

"Confound it, Sherlock, I wish you had consulted me before entrusting any such missive to that half-barbarous scarecrow scamp—"

Sherlock glanced at me with an unmistakable twinkle in his eye.

Mycroft ranted on, "—our uncouth sister, all mischief, like a rascally terrier pup barely house-broken—"

I could resist no longer.

"Now, now," I said in my normal and, alas, quite distinctive voice, "surely she is at least partially housebroken, and no more rascally, uncouth, or half-barbarous than other members of her family have sometimes showed themselves to be—"

As if he were a bellows, all the air seemed to exit Mycroft suddenly as he turned to gawk at me.

"—for instance, by speaking of such delicate family matters in the presence of a complete stranger," I concluded serenely, fully aware of my Gypsy bonnet at its fetching angle, my lovely pearl earrings, my ruffled collar starched to perfection. I gave him my most demure smile for a moment before I broke into a less ladylike grin.

"Enola?" gasped Mycroft.

"Yours truly, my dear brother."

"Enola! But—I never! What—how—where in the name of—"

But at that moment the cab stopped, and the cabbie bawled in a bored tone, "Kipple Street."

CHAPTER
THE
SIXTEENTH

Hopping out with my carpet-bag in hand, I opened it whilst Sherlock paid for the cab and sent it trotting off. Mycroft stood like a stump as I handed him a lantern and some matches. Having planned only for the company of one brother, not two, I kept the other lantern for myself; Sherlock was carrying his heaviest walking-stick, an excellent weapon. As he was managing Toby, I handed him Duquessa del Campo's handkerchief, then stuffed my Gypsy bonnet along with my gloves and my expensive wig into the carpet-bag, and covered my beacon of a yellow dress with a lightweight black cloak I had brought along for that purpose. Uniformly drab now, with my swamp-coloured hair in an untidy bun atop my head, I turned to my elder brother with a smile.

"Now, Mycroft, do I look more like your very own renegade sister?" As an afterthought, I peeled my little birthmark off my face and tossed it into the carpet-bag.

Mycroft seemed speechless—an unusual condition for him.

"So, Enola, where to start?" Sherlock asked me.

"Down along the Thames." Carpet-bag in one hand and lantern in the other, I led the way in that direction. "It seems to me," I explained, "that they would have brought her out of the Underground by one of the old sewers that the mud-larks and toshers use—"

"Her?" Explosively Mycroft regained his power of speech. "Whom—"

"Duquessa Blanchefleur del Campo," Sherlock enlightened him. "Enola, you think that after robbing her of her finery, they would have returned her to the ditches and docks?"

"I don't know. But certainly they could not keep her in the shop, could they?"

"Hardly." Something in Sherlock's tone made me think he took our search none too seriously, but was thoroughly enjoying himself. I, on the other hand, whilst amused by Mycroft's discomfiture, felt most determined to find the Duquessa.

Treading softly, silent and alert, I took us downhill, traversing a spiderweb of lanes that led to the river—although truth to tell, so pretty a word as *river* gives the wrong picture of the Thames, which was more like a stinking brown sewer that swelled or sank with the ocean tides. The brackish, sludgy water concealed drowned rats, dead cats, and, occasionally, decomposing human bodies. The banks were a rotting place where reptilian forms of humanity dwelt.

Heading down a steep, dark alley between buildings that smelled of tar, I hesitated, hearkening to a remembered fear. Sure enough, ahead we could see the vertical lines of ships' masts against the lighter gloom of a low sky, and we emerged from the alley to cluster on a rickety, rocking dock at the edge of the Thames.

Standing still for a moment, we all listened—and looked, to the extent of our lanterns' glow—for danger. "I have been here before," I whispered.

"When?" Sherlock asked, keeping his voice low.

"My first night in London." In less time than it takes to say it, I remembered those terrible hours held captive along with little Lord Tewksbury in the hull of a boat, my hands and feet tied, my wrists bloodied as I contrived to rub their bindings against one of the steel stays in my slashed corset. Then the fight for freedom, and then running, running through the night, slowed by poor Tewky with his sore, bare feet . . .

"What are you talking about?" Mycroft grumbled.

"I ran afoul of cutthroats hereabouts."

"How very comforting."

"This way," I whispered, turning randomly to my right, fleeing the memory. All along the shore loomed dark warehouses, visible only because of the glaring gas-brackets of corner taverns. Slimy, uneven footing ran along the river's edge. A villainous place. Just the sort of place where Mrs. Culhane and her thuggish friends might dump the unfortunate Duquessa. "Let us see what Toby can do with the handkerchief, Sherlock."

One of the things that I liked best about Sherlock was his way with dogs and horses. Regarding Toby, he stopped where he was and crouched to confer with him, caressing and cajoling interest into him before he pulled the square of fine lace-edged linen from his pocket and presented its centre to the dog's nostrils. When Toby had sniffed thoroughly, Sherlock arose and clipped a very long leash to the shorter one, giving him freedom. With an odd, waddling gait the dog trotted into the night, out of sight of our lanterns.

"Well, at least he is not leading us to you, Enola," Sherlock remarked as we followed the leash. "Your scent is on that handkerchief, you know."

"Yes. And yours. And Mrs. Culhane's."

"Confound it, Enola, there is something about

your presence that hampers my mental faculties. . . . We should have stopped at the Duque del Campo's residence and asked for something more redolent of the Duquessa's scent and hers alone."

"And what do you think they would have given you, her unlaundered drawers?"

"Enola!" Mycroft protested in crimson tones, for I had just mentioned unmentionables in his male presence.

I ignored him, badgering Sherlock. "For what purpose could you say you wanted such a personal item?"

"Explanation would have stirred up false hopes and entirely too many questions," he replied with a sigh. "You are quite right, Enola. Still, it will be a wonder if Toby does not take us to Mrs. Culhane's shop."

"It will be more than a wonder, nearly a miracle, if he finds anything to help us," I admitted. "But one must try."

"And I?" came a grumpy voice from the rear. "For what reason am I here really, Sherlock, pray tell?"

"All will become plain, my dear brother. All will become plain."

CHAPTER THE SEVENTEENTH

SEVERAL HOURS LATER, THIS BLESSED CLARITY HAD not yet occurred. With the characteristic willing optimism of canines, Toby led us stumbling along the littered, uneven edge of the Thames, hauling us into every conceivable gutter, stream, undercut, and sewer-mouth, but without satisfactory results. Indeed, he ended up leading us back the way we had come, towards the dockyard upon which centred my evil memories. Only Mycroft's wheezing, I am sure—for he was unaccustomed to physical exercise—kept him from complaining as we neared a tunnel, actually a dried-up river-bed, we had passed once before—

Toby alerted, but with his head in the air, not with his nose to the ground.

Other than that, I cannot explain my instant

alarm, although life on the streets does endow one with a certain warning sensitivity.

"Into the tunnel!" I whispered most vehemently, grasping each of my brothers by an elbow and propelling them thither. "Lanterns out!" There was no need to enquire regarding the dog, for as we stood close together in dense shadow, I felt Toby sitting on my feet, his furred body stiff, apprehensive.

There was no need to caution anyone to complete silence, except that I crouched to place a warning hand around Toby's snout.

We heard footsteps shuffling up the riverbank from the direction of the docks.

And voices.

Someone was approaching.

In a moment I heard two voices, one high-pitched and squeaky, the other deeper and huskier, with the phlegm of age in it, but still—a woman? And why did I think the squeaky soprano was a man? Both of them sounded familiar to me, although I could not place them.

Especially not as the deeper voice shocked me nearly witless by rapidly and angrily saying several exceedingly wicked words. ". . . 'ad me bellyful of 'er," it concluded.

"An' she of you, I reckon," retorted the squeaky voice.

"Then why in blazes don't she go away?" (I paraphrase, *blazes* being a euphemism in consideration of the sensibilities of the gentle reader.) "Every time I come out of my own 'ouse, there she is, just layin' like a fish in the filth of the mews—"

"Well, fair enough, for you put 'er there, dincha?" interrupted Squeaky.

Squeaky!

I nearly squeaked myself as I recognised the rat-like tones of the vicious little cutthroat who might have killed me last summer—

" 'At's got nuttin' to do wid it, you—" and oaths fit to char my ears interrupted my unpleasant memories. I would not have thought that any female could curse so, not even—

The two of them hove into view, rounding a bend in the riverside path, the larger, rather tortoise-shaped one carrying a lantern.

Not even Mrs. Culhane.

For unmistakably it was Mrs. Culhane, with the villainous Squeaky at her elbow.

"It is she," I hissed into Sherlock's ear, fervidly hoping he understood, for I dared say no more. Shuddering, I cringed deeper into the shadows. Mycroft had managed to quell his wheezing, thank goodness. He and Sherlock kept perfect silence as the two villains trod nearer.

". . . she 'as the 'ole neighbour'ood talking, an' dem all if word gits to the police," said Mrs. Culhane in conclusion to her ranting. The gentle reader will understand that I euphemise the few words fit to repeat. "The dem confounded troublemaker, stayin' around and playin' pitiful 'stead of runnin' 'ome like she oughter."

By this time they were walking nearly in front of our hiding place. I thought of the dagger sheathed in the busk of my corset, mentally preparing myself, for if one of them happened to glance our way as the light of their lantern fell on us, I would need to pull it out quite quickly.

"So wot d'ye want me to do about 'er?" asked Squeaky.

"Why, get rid of 'er!"

" 'Ow? Do ye mean plop 'er somewhere else, like, or do ye want me to do fer 'er?"

Kill her, he meant, and his offhand willingness made my neck-hair prickle. Luckily, it also made Mrs. Culhane look straight at him, and only at him, as the two of them passed our hiding place, and he was looking at her.

"Do wot you like," she told him. "I don't care. I don't want to know nothing about it. Just get rid of 'er."

"After them," I whispered once the evil twosome had passed our refuge. Indeed, Sherlock was already creeping forward. He wore the softest of kid-boots, always, and possessed a catlike grace upon his feet;

I did not fear they would hear him. I did, however, fear that they might hear me, for such situations seem to bring out the worst of my clumsiness. I gave Sherlock a good start before I followed, holding Toby's leash but leaving my lantern behind in case it might bang or rattle. Mycroft, taking his cues from me (amazingly!), did the same, trailing me at a discreet distance and treading, I am sure, most carefully, for our only light was that of London's gas-lamps hazily reflected from the low clouds, plus Mrs. Culhane's lantern far ahead.

Thus in dim, stealthy procession we trailed along the Thames for a short distance before veering away from it, uphill, towards the very place where we had started: that is to say, Kipple Street. Long before we got there I had guessed where we were going. I knew the mews behind Mrs. Culhane's shop from that same exceedingly unpleasant day the summer before, when I had fled past the cowshed, the donkey's ramshackle stable, the goat-pen, and through a squawking, honking morass of hen and goose in my desperation to escape from Squeaky and his even more fearsome cutthroat companion.

But first came Kipple Street, intermittently illuminated by the few street-lamps which remained unbroken. Reaching the pavement, rather than step out into the gas-light, Sherlock stopped in the shadow of the corner building to wait for me.

And, I suppose, Mycroft. But in my haste I had no thought for my stout, trailing brother. Peeping around the corner of the building, I watched Squeaky and Mrs. Culhane turn, a caricature of a promenading couple, onto Saint Tookings Lane. "I know how to cut them off. Come!" I panted to Sherlock, and with the dog by my side I darted straight across Kipple Street to the alley that led directly into the mews.

Behind me I heard someone, I think Mycroft, expostulate, "Disgusting! Has the girl gone mad?" For as is the nature of such alleys, this one was strewn with the odiferous dung of all the domesticated animals aforementioned and many more. A most undesirable place to slip and fall. I tried not to do so as I ran forward into what would have been nothing but stench and darkness if it were not for a glimmer of lantern-light approaching from Saint Tookings Lane. Mrs. Culhane—

I failed to complete the thought that she and her consort had taken the slightly longer way of better footing. I gasped.

In the faint light I could see a pale something—or someone, for it seemed to be a human personage—recumbent in the muck.

Motionless.

Indeed, as still and pallid as a shrouded corpse.

Dear God, if it was—Blanchefleur, frail filament of womanhood—was she yet alive?

CHAPTER THE EIGHTEENTH

I COULD NOT TELL!

Not even as, a moment later, Mrs. Culhane and her murderous companion walked into sight, then halted to stand over her. Not even as the light of their lantern fell full upon her could I discern any motion.

Running towards them, my footfalls muffled by the most unspeakable muck, I tried to hold my breath and listen, but I was not yet near enough; I could not hear what they said. But I saw Mrs. Culhane set down the lantern, turn, and leave at her usual waddling gait.

I saw that the form on the ground, whether alive or dead, was a woman, unusually slender, clad in nothing but a chemise.

I saw her move slightly as if attempting to lift her head.

Alive!

And I saw Squeaky draw his knife to kill her.

"No!" I shrieked, dropping Toby's leash to free my hands, increasing my already reckless speed to sprint towards him. "Stop!" Rapidly closing in on him, yet I was not near enough to restrain him by any means other than my voice. "Murder! Police!" And as he jerked around, quite startled, to look for the source of the commotion, I threw my carpet-bag—for lack of any better weapon—I hurled it with desperate force at his head.

He ducked, and it missed, of course, but it gave me enough time to come face-to-face with him, with my dagger drawn.

His lip drew back in a mongrel-dog snarl as we crouched, blades menacing, shuffling our feet in a slow circle. He recognised me. "You again. Ye're dead," he said.

"Help," implored a faint voice from the ground. "Please help me."

The distraction very nearly "did fer" me. As I glanced downward, Squeaky struck.

Too late I attempted to parry. The cutthroat's knife flashed towards my undefended neck—but at the crucial instant, a walking-stick descended with great force upon Squeaky's hand, and he cried out as his weapon dropped from his fingers. Within the next moment, Sherlock had a firm hold of the puny villain, twisting both of his arms behind his back.

I opened my mouth to thank my brother, but there was no opportunity, for just then a huge form in a truly hideous bonnet lunged at Sherlock's shoulders. Mrs. Culhane was back. Staggering from the impact of her weight, Sherlock very nearly fell. Alas, he lost his grip on his prisoner, who at once took to his heels. I tried to detach Mrs. Culhane from my brother; she swatted me aside and sent me sprawling. But someone nearly as large as she grasped her flailing arm. Mycroft wrenched her off of Sherlock, hurling her to her adipose posterior into the muck.

I failed to enjoy this scene to my satisfaction at the time, because my concern was all for another faint cry from the ground. Kneeling beside the lady, I grasped her filthy hand in mine. "Your Grace?"

Looking up at me, she nodded, and indeed, even layers of grime could not obscure the flowerlike beauty of her face, although her glorious tresses were gone, leaving only an inch or two of stubble stiffened by mud. It was Duquessa Blanchefleur.

"Help me," she whispered.

"We have come to do so," I assured her. "But what—are you injured?"

She shook her head.

Toby, that paragon of trackers (according to *The*

Sign of the Four), came over and sniffed the Duquessa without showing the slightest hint of recognition.

"Are you weak?" I asked the lady. "Starved?"

"No, not at all!" Her lovely eyes widened, quite earnest. "The paupers share their bread with me. The poorest of the poor, in rags, have pity on me."

Just the same, I produced one of the strengthening sugar candies I always carry with me and placed it into her mouth, as Sherlock crouched at her other side, and Mycroft. Of Mrs. Culhane, I saw nothing more. Apparently, she had wisely retreated.

"But I want to go home," Lady Blanchefleur said quite simply, her words rendered pitiful only by her circumstances. "Will you take me home?"

"We have come here for that purpose," said Sherlock. "May I assist you to sit up, my lady?"

"Oh, no. No, I cannot sit up, nor can I stand, not by myself." She seemed a trifle breathless, as if shocked, as if sitting up or standing by herself would be indecent. "Unless someone could possibly fetch me . . ."

Her words trailed away, and one could hear the blushing embarrassment in them. Averting her eyes from my brothers, she gazed at me imploringly.

"What?" asked Mycroft with far less than his usual gruffness. "What on Earth is it that you need?"

Wincing away from his question, she whispered

to me, "I tried to crawl . . . but even that was . . . impossible. My waist . . ."

And I remembered the diabolical corset I had seen hanging in Mrs. Culhane's shop.

Blanchefleur had worn such a corset, her ladies had told me, since childhood.

Indeed, I looked down upon a woman with the waist of a six-year-old. Never before had I actually seen the proof, but Mum had read to me from her Dress Reform journals of such — such mutilation —

"Ye gods with bunions!" I exploded, suddenly furious, although not at the unfortunate lady. I glared across her supine, shorn, and deformed body at my brothers. "I am sure she was sent to the very best boarding schools, Mycroft!"

"What on Earth —"

"Her poor waist, compressed to the extent that her personage has . . ." I could not remember the word *atrophied*, and this made me even angrier. "All her strength given up to fashion, so that now she cannot sit, stand, or walk unless she is encased in one of those infernal devices of torture!"

Lady Blanchefleur began silently but with eloquence to weep.

I have never seen Mycroft look so bewildered, but Sherlock, because he had at one time been subjected to quite a lecture by Florence Nightingale, did understand. Indeed, as one might expect, Sherlock took charge. "Hush, Enola. You've said enough. Might we borrow your cloak?"

Biting my lip to silence my anger, I stood up, took off the much-besmirched cloak, and handed it to him.

"Now, Your Grace, we shall carry you. Mycroft, lift her shoulders, please. There, you see, I told you our undertaking tonight would require two strong men."

Actually, once he had the Duquessa wrapped in my cloak for modesty, Sherlock carried her easily by himself, she was such a frail thing, her weight so slight. He turned westward, towards the City. But after we had tramped through the slums for quite a distance without seeing a cab—indeed it would have been difficult to find one anywhere in London, as the hour was perhaps four in the morning—he turned to Mycroft and said, almost as if they were two boys again playing a game, "Your turn. Here."

He handed the lady over to Mycroft, and to Mycroft's credit, he bore the burden gently and steadily.

Still we saw no cab nor any sign of any form of transportation. Certainly the East End streets were not deserted, not in summertime, but the drunkards and other denizens, sneak thieves and round-the-corner Sallys, stayed far from us: two grim aristocratic men carrying what appeared to be a lifeless body as I trailed along, quite a sight I am sure in my muddy yellow dress with my face, hands, and hair in a mess, carrying a carpet-bag and leading a spotted spaniel by a leash.

Mycroft eventually handed Duquessa Blanchfleur back to Sherlock, and so we continued for miles, as they took turns carrying her.

During this entire protracted ordeal, both of my brothers remained almost completely silent, and Sherlock, in the lead as usual, seemed to have forgotten that I existed. But Mycroft walked next to me, and I felt him stealing frequent glances at me.

At last he spoke. "Enola. When, earlier this evening, Sherlock told me that all would become plain, was he speaking of you?"

Actually, I had no idea why Sherlock had insisted on bringing Mycroft along. Therefore I had no answer for Mycroft's question. But as Mycroft seriously awaited my reply, sudden irrepressible laughter burst from me. "Indeed," I cried, "considering the condition of my hair, my face, and my personage right now, seldom has a woman been plainer."

I heard Sherlock chuckle. But Mycroft gazed at me, more solemn than ever, and in that moment, to my astonishment, I felt that I rather liked him.

"Exactly," he said. "Last summer I met a rather spoilt yet neglected stick of a girl, or so it seemed to me. Yet now I see quite an extraordinary woman. All is not plain, not at all, for you are still but fourteen years of age."

"Fifteen," I replied pensively, "in a few days." I had been thinking of my approaching birthday anniversary with no great joy.

Already owlish, Mycroft's eyes widened yet more. "Really?"

"Truly?" exclaimed Sherlock at the same time. "Has it been a year already?"

"Almost a year since Mum ran off with the Gypsies? Yes."

Saying it made me remember the message from Mum that I carried, still unread, over my heart, and I felt a familiar ache. Somewhat intensified, under the circumstances.

"I still cannot *believe* our mother would—" Mycroft began, for apparently Sherlock had discussed Gypsies with him.

But Sherlock silenced him. "I coerced you into accompanying us tonight, Mycroft," he told his older brother quietly, "so that you would come to know Enola better, see her in action, and perhaps derive some insight from the experience." Meaningfully, he halted, turned to Mycroft, and handed over to him the helpless and apparently fainting Duquessa Blanchefleur. "Have you?"

"This is an exceedingly inconvenient time for conversation," Mycroft growled.

"Quite," agreed Sherlock placidly as Mycroft trudged forward with his burden and we walked beside him. "At your earliest convenience, then?"

Mycroft said something rather naughty, although justifiable under the circumstances, which I shall not repeat.

Silently we slogged onward.

Chapter
the
Nineteenth

Dawn bleached the sky behind the chimney-pots by the time we finally reached Aldgate Pump, one of London's huge hygienic monstrosities, unofficial marker that we were passing out of the unwashed East End and into the City proper. At the adjacent cab-stand, a few yawning drivers had arrived, and Sherlock was able to secure a four-wheeler.

As he laid Duquessa Blanchefleur gently upon one of the seats, she stirred and opened her eyes. "It is as I have always thought," she murmured. "At their hearts, people are truly kind. Thank you."

"You deserve all kindness," I told her as I gave her another candy.

Nor did Sherlock disabuse her by reminding her of the "kindness" of Mrs. Culhane or Squeaky.

Instead, he turned to me. "Enola, might I ask you how you came to be involved in this affair?"

"Of course you may ask," I told him, and although we were all very weary from the night's labours, I hoped my smile expressed my fondness for him. "But I decline to answer."

He raised his eyes heavenward briefly before he spoke again. "Let me rephrase. You are known to Duque Luis del Campo and his household?"

"I am known to them as a concerned gentlewoman."

"Then I think it would be less distressing to the household if you and you alone were to see Duquessa Blanchefleur home."

"Leaving masculine eyes out of the matter, you mean."

"Exactly. Wait a minute." Taking Toby's leash from me and handing it to Mycroft, he strode to Aldgate Pump, produced a handkerchief (not edged with lace — his was the large masculine item), sopped it with water, came back to me, and began scrubbing my face as if I were a child.

Exceedingly fatigued, and also caught off guard, I stood like a department-store dummy for a few minutes before I reacted, pushing him away and taking the handkerchief to finish the job myself, washing mud and muck off my face and hands.

"Not too bad," Sherlock said doubtfully once I had put on my wig and my hat to cover my dreadful hair. "Do you need your birthmark?"

"No."

"Until we meet again, then."

"Yes. Once this errand is done, I quite intend to sleep until tomorrow."

I tossed my carpet-bag into the cab. But as I placed my foot on the step to follow it, Mycroft spoke for the first time. "Wait!"

Poor Mycroft, I had almost forgotten he was there. With hasty compunction I turned to him.

All of his usual pomposity and loquacity had vanished during the rigours of the night. He spoke with gruff but almost childlike simplicity. "When shall we see you?"

So warm was the unexpected surge of affection I felt for him that I had to remind myself that he had made no promises and I could not trust him. After a moment I replied, "I don't know. I will be in touch. I promise."

"Kindly notice that I have not summoned a constable to take you in hand," he replied with some return of his usual testiness.

"I have noticed, believe me," I told him earnestly.

"Such being the case, why can we not agree—"

"I am quite exhausted, Mycroft, unable to reason. I dare not agree to anything."

Suddenly Sherlock spoke up with incoherence most unusual for him. "Enola. Your birthday!"

I turned to him in genuine bewilderment. "My birthday? What of it?" Neither of them had ever concerned himself with my birthday.

And both of them seemed to have lost all of their usual eloquence. As if he were having trouble completing a thought, Sherlock said, "We should be together."

"What for?"

"All three of us," Mycroft said just as labouriously.

Not to celebrate, certainly, the day that our mother had run away. "I cannot imagine either of you offering me cake or gifts. Why . . ."

But I let the question incomplete, partly because it would have been cruel to make them say any more, partly because I myself could not at that time face my own befuddled emotions, and also because—odd, for a logician's daughter—I remembered what the Gypsy woman had said to me: that I was fated to be forever alone—unless I chose to defy the fate.

Together. All three of us.

Or safely alone?

The decision was mine.

"Enola?" asked Mycroft.

Far too tired to think it through, I trusted the impulse of my heart: I nodded. "Baker Street? Sherlock?"

"Baker Street by all means, at tea-time. Bring the skytales."

That simply it was decided: The three of us would meet again on — not so much my birthday as the anniversary of Mum's disappearance. All three of us trying to decipher what had become of her.

A bitter thought. But I said only, "Very well," and waved, and stepped into the cab to take Duquessa Blanchefleur home to Oakley Street.

I pillowed her exceedingly dirty and pitifully cropped head in my lap whilst holding her hand. A few times during the journey she opened her eyes, but only to give me her angelic smile and close them again.

When we reached the Duque's Moorish mansion, it was still very early, with only intermittent sleepy traffic on the street and pavements. Nevertheless, I knocked for the cabbie to descend, then told him to pull around to the back of the del Campo residence, like a delivery van. Fewer eyes would see there, and I felt sure that Duque Luis del Campo would prefer (as I did, for different reasons) that details of Blanchefleur's whereabouts whilst absent from her family should be kept out of the newspapers.

As we stopped by the kitchen door, a cook ran out, scolding, then screamed like a guinea hen when I opened the cab and she saw the scene within.

"Fetch your master," I told her, "and Mary —"

Heavens, I could not think of their names, only Mary of Magdala, of Bethany, of Nazareth, of flowers, none of which would do. "Send down Duquessa Blanchefleur's ladies-in-waiting, and hurry. And be quiet about it," I added futilely as she scuttled off squealing like a shoat.

The Duque appeared first. In days to follow I drew many amusing sketches of that noble gentleman, his black hair all in polliwogs, rushing out in his nightgown with his bony ankles and bare feet protruding beneath the hem; true to his hot-blooded nature he had not paused even to put on slippers or a dressing-gown. Then came—Mary in chenille and Mary in flannel; I still could not remember Hambledon or Thoroughcrumb or which was which, nor did it matter. They shrieked and wept. The Duque, to his everlasting credit in my mind, verily kissed his wife again and again upon her thoroughly besmirched face.

However, it did seem to me that more practical steps were in order. Paying the cabbie, I suggested to the Duque that he should take his wife inside, and he gathered her up and did so, bellowing at the cook to summon the doctor, whilst the two Marys and I trailed after him. He placed her, muck and all, on a fainting-sofa in the parlour—never before had I seen that item of furniture used for its stated purpose. Whilst the Marys ran for smelling-salts, hot water, and Heaven knew what else, the Duque flung himself about the room in operatic paroxysms of joy at his wife's recovery, wrath at the perpetrators of her disappearance and her pitiful state, prayerful gratitude, impatience for the doctor to arrive, indeed every possible reaction, only occasionally and incidentally including demands for explanations.

So eventually, as the Marys took over and the physician hurried in, I was able to excuse myself, having given only the most vague of accounts implying that Dr. Ragostin had located the lady, but in his masculine delicacy he preferred not to be credited in any way or mentioned in the affair. Duque Luis himself seemed overtaken by similar delicacy, although his might have been more of the societal variety; he asked me nothing of what I had seen or where Blanchefleur had been, and I felt sure that when he contacted Scotland Yard he would report only that his wife had been found and refuse any further cooperation. A headline would appear in the newspapers hailing the return of the Duquessa, but the text that followed would consist mostly of creative speculation. Sherlock Holmes, like Dr. Ragostin, would receive no credit in the affair.

Nor would my brother wish for any recognition, I thought as a different cab, innocent of mud, drove me away. In Dr. Watson's accounts of the great detective's adventures, Sherlock Holmes often declined to be mentioned in the solution of a case. Surely neither he nor Mycroft desired plaudits in this one.

Sherlock. Mycroft. I had brothers.

How odd it felt, how old-fashioned, how — comfortable.

I did not bother stopping my cab at the wrong place, ducking through Underground stations, any of my usual precautions in case I had been followed by either of the aforementioned brothers. I was simply too tired to bother. Also, to my muted surprise, I realised that, should they find out where I lived, I no longer cared. In short, I had the cabbie take me directly to the Professional Women's Club.

Once there, I staggered in by the side door so as not to make a mess of the receiving-room's carpeting, heaved myself upstairs to my room, ordered a bath and some buttered toast, partook of both, sent down my laundry, and, at about the time most folk were commencing their day's work, I collapsed into bed for, I blush not to say it myself, a very well-earned nap.

CHAPTER
THE
TWENTIETH

SLEEPING DURING THE DAY TENDS TO INDUCE CON-
fusion. I awoke that afternoon feeling quite young
and wretched, sure that I'd slept right through my
birthday and therefore received no worthwhile pres-
ents, on top of which Mum had gone missing, I had
hunted for her through the woods of Ferndell in the
rain, and now my knickerbockers were wet but I
needed to meet my brothers at the train station — my
brothers! No wonder I felt so frantic. I had never
met them. I wanted them to find my mother, but also
I did very much want them to like me. I must not
wear knickerbockers, my hair dreadfully needed
washing, all my white frocks had grass stains on
them, and what if I couldn't make it to the train station in time on my bicycle —

Bicycle?

Absurd. I hadn't ridden a bicycle in a year. I had abandoned mine in a copse of trees on a hill overlooking the country town of Belvidere during my own flight to London.

Sitting up, recognising my room in the Professional Women's Club, realising that my birthday was not until tomorrow but I must indeed meet my brothers, in a sense for the first time, wearing a nice frock — then I saw that I had left a brown impression on my pillowcase. My hair *did* dreadfully need washing.

How peculiar, the parallels between last year and this. As I got out of bed to ring the bell for service, I still felt befuddled, as if I had slept late and missed seeing my mother depart, I must find her, notify the constabulary in Kineford village, I must at once take my bicycle —

Bicycle.

There it was again. Something tapping me on the shoulder.

Mum had taken quite a bit of trouble to teach me to ride a bicycle, now that I thought about it, and that was extraordinary, for Mum had not generally troubled herself much about me. "You will do very well on your own, Enola" had been her usual daily dismissal.

Hmm.

Evidently the ability to ride a bicycle had been important to Mum, Suffragist and reformer that she was. Indeed, standing on a cold floor barefoot in my nightgown and recalling various conversations, I realised that a bicycle was a symbol of sorts for Mum's beliefs: A bicycle offered freedom of movement to females whilst defiantly flaunting the fact that they were, indeed, bipeds, just like those who wore trousers.

Very likely Mum assumed that I had my bicycle here with me in London. She probably thought that I had ridden it here.

Oh. Oh, my wheeling stars.

I felt weak (excusably so, considering how little I had eaten lately) and sat down on the bed, clutching its edge with both hands.

The bicycle. The skytales. Undeniably a bicycle incorporated various tubular, cylindrical parts of considerable size. Not only that, but it seemed to me—thinking of the many bicycles I had seen—it seemed that they were all made of metallic cylinders of approximately the same dimensions.

Certainly it was worth a try. But I simply could not deal with it yet. I needed to wash my hair—quite a bother, as it required a fire in the hearth, numerous warmed towels, and the assistance of a maid—and it needed to dry, which took hours. Also, the pain and commotion in my middle nearly bent me double; I badly needed something restorative to eat. I would be fully occupied for what remained of the day, and

I had no idea where to find a bicycle, other than perhaps by stopping a messenger-boy in the street.

However, after a soothing soup, some heavenly fresh-baked bread, hot shepherd's pie, and a cup of divine tapioca custard—after taking dinner in my room because my hair was not yet dry, I could better think what to do.

I applied myself to ink, pen, and my best writing paper, with the following result:

My dear brother,

You will find this an odd birthday request, I am sure, but it is of utmost importance, not only to me but to you and Mycroft. If you would be so good, I would like you to borrow or otherwise obtain several "dwarf" safety bicycles such as the one I used to ride, so that I may attempt an experiment upon them at tea-time.

I know you will not fail me.

Fondly,
Your seditious sister,
Enola

I addressed this to Sherlock Holmes but included no return address, and rather than trust a messenger, I simply delivered it myself, with my hair in a bun, large dark glasses on my nose, and wearing the nondescript hat and tweeds of a spinster, thereby attracting no unpleasant attention on the Underground—a danger at this late hour. Everyone was abed when I slipped my note through the slot in the door of 221 Baker Street. Sherlock would receive it in the morning.

The morning of my fifteenth birthday, forsooth.

And I spent most of the morning, indeed most of the day, in preparation for my birthday tea. I decided upon a fashionably cut (puffed shoulders, indeed) gown of plum-coloured nainsook, that is to say, the very finest cotton, beautifully draped, suitable for summertime weather yet as luxurious as silk. And I took a risk: Rather than wear my trusty wig, I asked one of the maids at the Professional Women's Club to help me with my own freshly laundered hair. A doughty woman, rising to the challenge, she gave it no less than five hundred strokes with a hairbrush in an attempt to smooth it and render it glossy. Perversely, it chose instead to fly skyward in all directions, but she was not intimidated, and with the assistance of water and numerous hairpins she tamed it into a very presentable chignon. With some discreet colour added to my face, collar and under-sleeves of ruffled white cotton appended to my plum nainsook frock, and golden-yellow day lilies upon my hat and bodice, I was more satisfied than surprised to find, upon checking myself in the standing full-length mirror, that I passed muster right down to the shine on my dove-coloured button-top boots; even Mycroft could find nothing less than ladylike in my appearance.

This comforted me little; my sentiments concerning today's meeting with Mycroft—taking tea, forsooth!—were considerably confused and more than a little frightened. Recalling that bleached dawn and Mycroft's solemn, weary face, his fatigue shared with mine, my feelings, my thoughts about the Gypsy's words—it all seemed nonsensical now, how affectionately and impulsively I had agreed to meet him. Ludicrous, that I should go like a lamb to risk my freedom. I had given my word and I would keep it, but still . . . *Gypsy superstition! Really, Enola,* I chided myself as I found the dove-coloured gloves that matched my boots, surveyed myself in the mirror one more time, sighed, then went down to hail a cab.

Only my gloves kept me from biting my fingernails during the brief cab ride.

But the instant we stopped at 221 Baker Street, my thoughts were thoroughly diverted, for upon the pavement in front of my brother's lodging stood quite an impressive array of bicycles.

Also upon the pavement stood my brothers, both of them, but they failed to seize my interest. The moment I had paid the cab-driver, I turned to the bicycles, my gaze darting from one to the next.

"What ever is she about?" Mycroft demanded.

I heard a shrug in Sherlock's voice as he replied, "Bicycles she wanted, and bicycles she shall have."

"This one!" I exclaimed, belatedly raising my head to greet my brothers. "Hello, Mycroft. Hello, Sherlock." I grasped the bicycle's handle-bars, rolling it forward for better access, then began to strip off my gloves to get to work. "This particular one looks very much like the ones Mum and I used to ride. Not that any of them vary greatly in dimensions. But I think we should try this one first." I drew Mum's coded message, the skytale, from my bosom, the feminine carryall that was considered safer than pockets.

"Ah! There is method in her madness!" With great good spirit Sherlock echoed the phrase that had often been applied to himself.

I failed to catch Mycroft's reply, for I was all intent on the bicycle. The long column that ran down from the handle-bars towards the pedals seemed most likely for a skytale. However, after winding one of my strips of paper a few times around it, I saw that it was not going to give satisfaction. I muttered something rather naughty.

"Really, my dear sister," said a masculine voice near my shoulder, causing me to startle most provokingly; I had not noticed that my brothers had walked over to stand behind me. My irritation subsided instantly, however, as I realised with amazement that the words, gentle and teasing, had been spoken not by Sherlock, but by Mycroft.

Indeed, Sherlock sounded the more pompous of the two today. "Applying analysis of our mother's character to the problem," he pontificated, "one would think that, to her, the most important part of a bicycle would be the mechanism upon which the rider exerts control."

As my back was turned to him, I allowed myself to roll my eyes before shifting my attention to the thick metal column running up to the handle-bars.

Quickly I forgot to be annoyed with Sherlock, for as I wound the skytale spiraling up that cylinder, I saw words beginning to form. But I could complete the message only by winding the paper to its end, just beneath the bicycle's handle-bars, and even then I could read only a few lines:

. . . cannot be a mother without first being a person; family, husband, and children should not be allowed,

*as is so often the case, to steal a
woman's selfhood and her dreams.
I considered that, if I were not
true to myself, then all the
mothering I could give you would
have been falsehood. . . .*

My brother Sherlock, crouching on the other side of the bicycle, continued reading around the curve of the cylinder:

*I cannot be other than who I am,
but perhaps I should not have been
a mother. Such being the case, I
find it no surprise that your brothers
are both bachelors; . . .*

"Heavens," Mycroft said. "Quite an epistle, and I believe we have got hold of it by the middle. There are three other strips of paper, are there not? Might we attempt to ascertain which comes first?"

"We might, indeed," Sherlock agreed, "and if you would be so good as to send the page-boy for pencil and paper, you can copy it down as Enola and I read it out to you."

Thus my birthday "tea" began on the pavement outside 221 Baker Street. I will spare the gentle reader the full details of our fumblings and experimentations with the four strips of paper. I must say that I felt an unusual contentment, even joy of a sort, simply working together with my brothers towards a shared goal. My happiness, however, took a rude blow when we finally located the beginning of Mum's message:

My dearest Enola,
*   If you have received this communication, it means that I am deceased.*

CHAPTER
THE
TWENTY-FIRST

I WAS READING ALOUD AT THE TIME, AND MY VOICE faltered. Utter silence fell between the three of us, although the traffic in the street rumbled as loud as ever. Neither Sherlock nor Mycroft seemed to know what to say. Or perhaps they were waiting for me, dearest Enola, to speak.

"Of course," I said finally. "The charcoal markings on the envelope, the borders and encirclement and the guardian eyes — the Gypsies put them there to protect themselves whilst they delivered the message."

"In their superstition, they needed to ward off the shadow of death," said Mycroft gruffly. "Quite."

"Enola," said Sherlock, "I am sorry."

"For what?" Through the bicycle spokes I made what I hoped was a comical face at him. "Happy birthday to me."

Sherlock averted his eyes. "Billy," he called sharply to the boy-in-buttons, "you may return the rest of these bicycles to their owners."

Whilst he did so, we continued. Again, to spare the gentle reader I will not describe our continuing struggles with Mum's farewell missive. Here it is as Mycroft eventually transcribed it, in its entirety:

My dearest Enola,

If you have received this communication, it means that I am deceased. Abrupt and, indeed, cruel as those words may sound, I refuse to soften them by saying I have "passed on to a better place" or any of the usual platitudes. You know that as an educated woman and a freethinker I do not believe in a hereafter. One reason I have so ardently championed women's rights is because I am convinced that one's life is the only life one

shall ever have, and one should live
it to the fullest.

It was for this reason that I left
you—yes, I will say it; abandoned
you; do please believe I feel
appropriate guilt—in such a callous
manner. I meant to delay a year
or two longer, but I could feel a
very likely cancerous growth in my
abdomen enlarging at an alarming
rate, and I realised I had no time
to wait. Enola, you have always
been wise beyond your years, so I
hope you will be able to see that one
cannot be a mother without first
being a person; family, husband,
and children should not be allowed,
as is so often the case, to steal a
woman's selfhood and her dreams.
I considered that, if I were not

true to myself, then all the mothering I could give you would have been falsehood. I cannot be other than who I am, but perhaps I should not have been a mother. Such being the case, I find it no surprise that your brothers are both bachelors; perhaps you, also, will decline to beget children, and perhaps that would be for the best.

In any event: All of my life since I was a child I have longed to experience the simple freedom of the Gypsies. I love their colourful, comfortable dress, their singing violins, their head-tossing horses, their laughter, their flaunting of foolish rules. Their thievery, as you may well imagine, troubles me not at all, being in the same rebellious spirit as my own. For surely you know now that I was larcenous in the eyes of the law when I left you.

Doing so, I selfishly pursued my dream—but I offer the feeble excuse that I was also conscious of you, wishing to spare you the melodrama of deathbed attendance, black crepe and all of society's deplorable, onerous rituals of mourning. Also, I wished to avoid the fate of your poor father: a churchyard funeral and slab of stone. I wanted only to be free. Free in my life, what remained of it, and free in death.

How ironic, then, that I, a rationalist, have chosen to live out my days with people who fervidly believe in all sorts of nonsense, from palmistry to the afterlife. But despite their superstitions, nothing can lessen my affection for the Gypsies. They treat me almost as a deity. I lie now in a tent erected especially for me because I am dying. I am cared for tenderly even though those who touch me must undergo ritual cleansing afterward. New shoes are being made for me, and new clothing, so that I will have everything I need in order to be dead. Amulets and coins will be sprinkled on me when they lay me in the ground, and doubtless they will bury my paintbrushes with me. If I had horses or a caravan of my own, the caravan would be burned and the horses killed to go with me. As I do not, they will make wreaths shaped like horses and a caravan, and lay these upon my grave, which will be located wherever the wind has blown them at the time. After which, within a day, they will leave me behind, go on their wandering way, and go on singing.

To me, for reasons I cannot explain, this all seems quite beautiful. To you, perhaps not. I try to look at what I have done from your point of view and I realise I have surely caused you pain. Very likely you have wondered about my feelings for you as a mother. I myself have questioned whether I have given you all of the nurture that I could. Thankfully, the answer is _yes_; I loved you as well as I am able, being the person I am.

The paradox is that a different
mother would likely have given you
warmer love. But if you were the
daughter of a different mother, then
you would not be Enola.

Enola Eudoria Hadassah
Holmes, my daughter of whom I
am justifiably proud, I write this to
you because I owe you truth. To
your brothers I owe nothing. Yet
I rejoice in their accomplishments,
and I hope that, should the time
come when it is possible, you will
share the contents of this letter with
them.

I intentionally include no date.
I desire no anniversary
remembrance of my death.

It has been said that we "live on"
in the memories of those we leave

behind. With no desire to live on in any sense of the phrase, but trusting that you will not think too badly of me.

Your mother,
Eudoria Vernet Holmes

Our reactions to this epistolary event were interestingly various. Sherlock suddenly decided that he must himself return the remaining bicycle to its owner, and off he went, riding upon it, whilst Mycroft escorted me upstairs, puffing and very red in the face, then went down again, roaring for tea. As for me, I suppose I would not have been human had I not shed a few tears, especially when Reginald Collie came bounding to meet me, his whole-hearted, selfless affection in such contrast . . . I slumped on a sofa, the dog leapt to my side, and I laid my face against his furry neck and wept. If only my mother had been more like a dog.

The absurdity of which thought almost made me laugh amidst my tears. *Now really, Enola,* I chided myself, sitting up to blow my nose. Truly, I owed a great deal to my mother, and as she hoped, I did not think too badly of her. By being herself, Suffragist and troublemaker Eudoria Holmes, she had given me the courage of her example, to be myself: Enola.

Returning to find me wet-eyed, Mycroft rumbled a series of unintelligible tsking sounds and began to hunt in his pockets, but I was able to smile and tell him, "For a change I have my own handkerchief," holding up a dainty one embroidered with violets.

"All but useless," he grumbled.

"I think it has served its purpose." I no longer felt much inclined to weep. Rather, I marvelled to find myself sitting in the same room with my brother Mycroft without terror. I was astonished to see him obviously ill at ease, as I regarded him with fond amusement.

"Where is Sherlock, and where is the confounded tea?" he complained.

Whatever would we do without tea? It arrived, Mycroft poured, he offered me a plate of cake—birthday cake?—and as I took a slice he said suddenly, "Enola, I think it is within my power to make your birthday a bit happier after all."

"You already have," I said.

Crossly he responded, "Let me speak. First, I am sorry—"

"No need!" I cried.

"*Do* please be silent. I am sorry I ever heard of, or spoke, the words *girls' boarding school,* and given what I have lately learned, I no longer harbor any desire to send you to any such place. Moreover, I regret that I have so underestimated you. When we first met, I thought of you as a child I must save from herself, a responsibility I must undertake, indeed, a neglected waif to be rescued. Your response, although I have often found it outrageous, has nevertheless proved me quite mistaken." He had spoken largely to the tea-things, but suddenly he raised his piercing gaze, facing me directly from under his bristling eyebrows. "I hope you understand that I meant no harm."

"Of course you meant no harm. You were trying to do what you perceived as your duty." I realised we were about to enter into a diplomatic negotiation. Mycroft still held legal power over me, still felt responsible for me, and Sherlock was nowhere nearby to save me should Mycroft choose to take me quite literally in hand—yet, without mindfully knowing why, I felt not the least bit afraid.

Mycroft nodded. "What I still perceive as my duty. Enola, it is my responsibility to see that you live in a safe place—"

"I lodge at the Professional Women's Club," I told him, feeling sure it was no longer necessary to hide from him my whereabouts, although I still could not have said why.

His eyebrows shot up in amazed approval. "Nowhere in London could you be safer. But the expense! By now, the money our dear but devious mother provided for you—"

"I invested some of it in a boarding-house," I told him, "and the rents quite suffice for my needs."

"Good heavens!" he exclaimed, whilst just as explosively Reginald Collie barked and leapt about as our brother walked in. "Sherlock, did you hear that?" Of course Sherlock could not have heard any of it. With heavy momentum, rather like a mill-wheel, Mycroft turned to him. "She lodges at the Women's Club! She owns a boarding-house, and lives off the rents!"

"Why should you be surprised, my dear Mycroft?" Dropping into a chair as if the day's events had wearied him, Sherlock poured himself some tea. "You expected such competence; indeed, you are quite right in what you have been telling me all along."

"What do you mean?"

"You hypothesised that she was in the business of finding missing persons." Sitting back with cup in hand, Sherlock turned to me with a quizzical look. "The boarding-house you own, Enola—would it by any chance include the office of one Dr. Ragostin, Scientific Perditorian?"

I am afraid my smile deserted me. "How long have you known?"

"Only since I went to inquire of Duque Luis del

163

Campo whether his wife was feeling better, and he credited Dr. Ragostin with finding her." Sherlock seemed to find his tea remarkably invigorating, for now his eyes sparkled and his voice swelled, vibrant, as he said, "The upstart girl is my competition, Mycroft!"

Because he could not follow, Mycroft responded peevishly, "Sherlock, do please present your thoughts in some sensible order."

But Sherlock had turned to me. "Ivy Meshle worked as Dr. Ragostin's assistant?"

I sighed. "No, merely as his secretary. I have since promoted myself to assistant. Under another name."

Catching the conversational tiger by the tail at last, Mycroft sat up and ogled me. "You invented this Dr. Ragostin?"

"Exactly."

"So that you could devote yourself to finding missing persons?"

For a moment I could not reply; there seemed to be a warm obstruction in my throat. Both pairs of brotherly eyes were fixed on me, each exhibiting the same earnest desire to understand this strange creature, their sister, and in that moment I realised why I was no longer afraid of them.

They cared for me.

And I for them.

How—how delightful, how filling, how sweet was this knowledge—better than any birthday cake ever.

It enabled me to confide in them. "Yes, missing persons and things. I meant at first to find Mum—but I kept putting it off. . . ."

"Wise," Mycroft said with a nod.

"One must know oneself," said Sherlock softly. "How much one can take upon oneself. What one can bear."

For a moment we all sat quite silent, and I daresay we were all three thinking of our mother, whom we loved, I suppose, as well as we were able, being the persons we were.

Mycroft was first to rouse himself. "So, Enola," he asked, "what now? How can I best 'nurture' you, as our dear departed mother would say, and keep you from getting yourself killed, but no longer incur your enmity? Sherlock says you would like some higher education."

"I would," I admitted, "and I would like, for a change, to breathe air that has neither a greasy texture nor any visible smoky colour—"

"You would like to take a holiday from London?"

"For a while. Perhaps a few weeks in Ferndell." Reginald Collie leaned warm against my skirt as absentmindedly I stroked him. "Also, I would very much like to call on Lady Cecily Alistair and see

165

how she does, and whether we might be friends. Perhaps she might even consent to be a lady scholar along with me."

"A very good idea," said Mycroft, who knew something of my affection for Cecily. "And after that?"

"I will let you know. I need time to think. But, my dear brothers, both of you . . ." Sitting up, I engaged both pairs of hawk-grey eyes at once. "Please allow yourself no illusions of my ever becoming a traditional woman. Finding the lost is my passion, my life's calling. I *am* a perditorian."

"Excellent!" cried Sherlock.

"Scandalous," grumbled Mycroft in a resigned tone.

"Enola." Sherlock addressed me with as much emotion as one was ever likely to perceive in him. "My cherished sister, I beg of you, be whatever you like. Selfishly, I have become quite addicted to you, your flair—the zest of never knowing—truly, I cannot wait to see what on Earth you will do next."